Almost Touching
A Reader for Women and Men

Edited by Margo LaGattuta

Plain View Press
P. O. 33311
Austin, TX 78764
512-441-2452

The cover mosaic *"Almost Touching You,"* © 1996, was created in collaboration by the eleven writers and their editor. Visual artist and writer Lori Solymosi facilitated group sessions in her studio so that each writer could mold and glaze individual ceramic tiles. The center tile and design arrangement of the finished mosaic were created by Lori. The original artwork is owned by the group and exhibited at readings so that audiences can see and touch the power of collaboration—how the whole is greater than the sum of its parts.

Photographs of writers courtesy of Rick Ballantyne, Rick's Photography, 333 1/3 Main Street, Rochester, MI.

Detailed Photoshop work for the cover by Mark Ely.

Acknowledgments

The authors wish to acknowledge prior publication of the following pieces which appear in this book: *"Silent Expectations,"* **Embracing the Fall,** © 1994 Margo LaGattuta, Plain View Press; *"Mercury,"* **Touchstone Journal,** © March/April 1996 John Milam; *"Power of Three,"* Second Place in **Art in the Air Poetry Contest,** Fall 1995 Mike Jones; *"Original Oil"* and *"Power of Three,"* **HalfTones to Jubilee,** © Summer 1996 Mike Jones; *"Order Toll Free"* **Amphibious Maneuvers,** © 1996, Linda Sienkiewicz; *"Tied,"* **Touchstone,** Viterbo College, © 1995 Linda Sienkiewicz; *"Nightly Grind"* (Titled: *"Bruxism"*), Honorable Mention, **National Federation of State Poetry Societies,** 1995 Linda Sienkiewicz; *"All -Night Movie"* (Titled: *"Dirty Dishes"*), **Free Focus,** © 1996 Linda Sienkiewicz; *"Anaconda,"* Second Place in **Writer's Voice Tri-County Poetry Contest,** Spring 1996 Linda Sienkiewicz; *"Coming Off Zoloft,"* **Muddy River Poetry Review,** © 1996 Linda Sienkiewicz; *"Danger in Perfect Order,"* **Freedom Writer's Unite,** © 1996 Linda Sienkiewicz; *"Girlfriend,"* **Buffalo Bones,** © 1996 Linda Sienkiewicz; *"Kiss the Sun,"* **Freedom Writer's Unite,** © 1996 Linda Sienkiewicz; *"Running with that Dream,"* **Free Focus,** © 1996 Linda Sienkiewicz; *"Tattooed,"* **Freedom Writer's Unite,** © 1996 Linda Sienkiewicz; *"Wedding Ring,"* and *"Pushing Up the Screen,"* **Speakeasy V,** © 1995 Karen Renaud; *"Resolution and Good Intentions,"* **Lake Orion Eccentric, Oxford Eccentric,** © December 1995 Karen Renaud; *"Beyond Stillness,"* *"Surrender the Fall,"* **Speakeasy VI,** © 1996 Karen Renaud; *"Life in the Music,"* **The Blues Review,** © 1996 Karen Renaud; *"Seashell,"* **Abbey,** © 1993 Anita Elaine Page; *"Mammogram,"* **Womanwise,** © 1995 Anita Elaine Page; *"Smoothed,"* **The Mature American,** © 1995 Anita Elaine Page; *"Being Eight,"* **Parnassus Literary Journal,** © 1996 Anita Elaine Page; *"Reading Rumi,"* **Touchstone Journal,** © Dec/Jan 1996 Linda Angér; *"The Afterlife of Roses,"* **Touchstone Journal,** © Feb/Mar 1996 Linda Angér; *"Heroin"* and *"Wallpapering,"* **Freedom Writer's Unite,** © Feb 1996 Linda Angér; *"Between the Leaves,"* **Living the HAllife,** © Spring 1996 Linda Angér; *"Recipes,"* **Touchstone Journal,** © Dec/Jan, 1996 Linda Angér; *"Just Say No,"* **Metro Times,** © August 1994 David Sabbagh; *"Supersaturation,"* **Touchstone Journal,** © May/June 1996 David Sabbagh.

Contents

Foreword

Margo LaGattuta

I sit looking out my dining room window at the light snow falling. A cardinal perches on a branch almost touching the deck. He is a sign of wonder for me, a sign that something miraculous is about to happen. I feel a sense of beauty in the moment. The scene is so still, yet filled with expectancy. A powerful new book is being born.

Inside, the chairs around my oak dining table are empty, yet there is an electric energy present in this room. Eleven writers have spent a year of Sunday afternoons here — creating, sharing, honing and editing the sections in this book. There were joys and sorrows in the experience and, as the work is being published, I am again in awe of the creative power of community.

I chose these eleven writers for their talent, writing skill, and literary vision. I also chose them because their work represents a wide variety of experiences. I imagined a book that would explore deeply human challenges — physical, emotional, personal and universal. The poetry and prose in *Almost Touching* explores such diverse situations as recovering from cancer and closed head injury, attending a school for the blind, managing depression, and healing from a miscarriage. It deals with gender issues and relationships, joys and sorrows, and the whimsy of everyday life.

These are professional, published writers who, for the most part, didn't know each other when the book began. They have amazingly various day-jobs: letter carrier, house appraiser, artist, retired school principal, computer analyst, accountant, union activist, school bus driver, etc.. They met in my home studio every other Sunday. Through ten months of sharing, writing and critiquing, their poems and stories took shape. The creative process allowed for continuous growth in each writer. Sharing their lives on the page and meeting the challenges of editing and revision, they became a powerful team of collaborators.

They gave each other courage and validation, both difficult to find in the solitary act of writing. When life seemed to take precedence over art, the writers were encouraged by their peers to continue writing in spite of any personal struggles. When deadlines were approaching, each member faced his or her own demons. Is this really good enough? Will my family reject me when they read this? Can I stand to see this in print? The deadlines also allowed the collaborators to rise to the occasion with their very best work. All are talented writers, but each has a particular specialty. The group always saw the power of each participant's work, sometimes clearer than the writers could see for themselves.

As they wrote, from the heart, of the experiences of being a woman or a man in this world today, the writers began to weave a poignant tapestry of human renewal. *Almost Touching* travels through the darkest experiences to name and then transform them. It is a reader for women and men. I believe it stands as a strong testimony to the power of the human spirit to recover from the many challenges we face in our lives. It shows that, as we celebrate and name our diversity, we can emerge *almost touching* that place of wholeness where we are alike. We hope that you, the reader, can find your own stories in the selections presented here. Coming together through our shared moments, we can all feel a little less alone.

I want to thank Susan Bright, publisher of Plain View Press in Austin, Texas, for the opportunity to select manuscripts and edit this anthology. It is my second collection in the ongoing regional issue-based literary series called "New Voices" published by the press. My first, *Variations on the Ordinary, A Woman's Reader*, was published in 1995. Susan's dedication to truthful literary publishing, social change and personal freedom has inspired me. Her input on the book, as collaborative editor, gave me courage and support when I faced my own demons or feelings of uncertainty.

I want to thank the eleven writers: John, Bethany, Mike, Linda, Mary-Jo, Lori, Karen, Anita, Linda, David and Polly for bringing so much joy to my Sundays, and for reminding me again and again of the power of collaboration. We reached for the miraculous and found it over cheddar cheese and crackers. And I want to thank my grandson, Marcus Anthony, for being a writing prompt on my dining room table when he was just a week old. I saw the birth of this book in his brand new eyes.

SILENT EXPECTATION

There is a gentle rising up
in the fertile energy of the human
heart, a movement so subtle and moist
it may take weeks to transform
itself to green stem and bud,
but hour by silent hour it stirs
within the darkened loam
an electric possibility,
a great and precious hope
that breaks through crusted
barren soil, with the very momentum
of expectation, into red tulip.

© 1994, Margo La Gattuta, *Embracing the Fall*

*For those who
are reaching,
touching, or
almost touching. . .*

John Milam

Snagged Earthward

On Writing

> Writing is something I do.

> Writing is art.

> Art is, to me, the expression of a person's soul
> in the physical world.

I grow when I write. That is how it feels, although I stay the same. I become more aware of who I am and how I fit into the web of existence. My consciousness grows. As I write without judgement or fear (of not making sense or of writing something others won't understand), I find that two former enemies within myself, the slave of linear logic and the artist, work together. I can say what I feel and feel what I say.

Night

John Milam

Back in the cavern of myself,
I pick through cobwebs,
jostle piddling spiders to life.
They scurry warmly in the transient light,
casting monstrous shadows.

I kindle further
the closely drawn company of night
with a star,
snagged earthward
by a deftly placed grab.

Held near my face,
it burns through my palms and flies off,
kissing the earth
goodbye
on its querulous way.

John Milam

The Knife

Between bristling reeds and fencing flies,
minnows darted below the algae
as the taut-jawed alligator waited in a steamy swamp.
Hunters silently took aim
for the skin of a knife-case
that lies dead on a table in Michigan.

The knife swims in a boy's pocket
amid hoarded treasure:
gum to engage his free-floating mind
while Mrs. Brandquist expounds on History,
a lighter to ignite discoveries in after-school scientific fieldwork,
an unknown key to open undiscovered doors,
paper-clips for clandestine operations:
formed correctly, a stinging projectile
when fired from a rubber-band,
or instant classroom power-failure if bent into a U-shape,
held between books, and plugged into an outlet.

The seam wraps around the knife-case
like the belt on his mother's Singer
that connects the motor to the spindle.
That old sewing machine is made of steel.
She can see its machinery, its pulleys and levers,
as the wheel spins, the belt turns, and the needle goes
up and down
up and down
as she guides the material to sew up the hem
of a new curtain for his sister's bedroom window.

Trickle

John Milam

I build cities to scrape the ceiling
of a dimly lit, closed-off room.
No one can intrude
and destroy.
Limits only of time
and space
and natural reality:
No sun
No snow
No warm, radiant tropics
No sandstorms.

Steady unmarred grim existence
between grime-bespottled walls . . .

until I'm driven out
into the turmoil
and the constant exposure
makes my head ache
from inside out
and I'm bent to breaking
supported by my vision
of safety
of home
until I'm there again,
only to go out
and do it all over again.

I burst in the face of the world
and trickle down.

John Milam

July 9, 1984:
Good Morning, Long Beach

(Excerpt from the first chapter of "Toward Acceptance,"
an autobiographical novel still in progress)

Melissa pushed him around the corner by the reception desk and down the bare hall he'd seen when he first came in. Just before they got to an elevator, they turned left into a small, bare-walled, windowless office. She parked him in front of the desk, then walked around it and sat down. She took a sheet of paper out of her portfolio. He could see, through the back before she set it down on the desk, that it was covered with black lines and a small amount of print at the beginning of some of the lines.

"I'm just going to check the basic information we have and make sure it's right. Is your name Jeremy Cochran?" He nodded.

"You live at 34679 Shoshone, in Lake Forest?"

He didn't know that address. He shook his head. He knew his real address, and he could have told her what it was if he could have spoken.

"Do you live at 8573 Westwood Court, Birmingham, Michigan?"

He nodded vigorously and grinned at the familiar address. His family's mailing address had been Birmingham although, according to a map, they lived in Bloomfield Township. That had always confused everyone, and he was glad he didn't have to explain it to her. But he seemed unable to stop grinning, even though he wanted to. His face wouldn't relax.

"Do you remember moving?"

His attention went to this new question, and his face relaxed. He thought about their house in Michigan. He couldn't remember moving anywhere. He shook his head.

"You live in California now. You live in Lake Forest, a Los Angeles suburb. This hospital is Long Beach Memorial. You're in the rehabilitation unit." She paused for a minute. "Do you remember working at [she looked at the paper in front of her] Cass Spars?"

He shook his head. He had seen ads for Cass Spars in sailing magazines (a spar was part of a sailboat that supported the sails—a mast, boom, or spinnaker pole), but could he really have worked there and not be able to remember it?

"You were hurt in an accident when you were working. Something fell on your head. Do you know what day it is?"

He shook his head again.

"It's Monday, July 9. Do you know what year?"

He thought, 1983. But now he wasn't sure of anything, so he shook his head.

"It's 1984. Do you remember going to college at [she looked at the form] Michigan Technological University?"

A picture of the small upper peninsula campus of Michigan Tech formed in his mind. It was the picture on the cover of the pictorial book from the annual winter carnival at MTU. They held the carnival every February. Students participated in ice sculpture contests, hockey, basketball, and "broomball" tournaments (a cross between ice hockey and soccer that was played on a snow-covered field with a goal at each end), talent shows, and a contest for Winter Carnival King and Queen. Jeremy remembered the "dogsled" races he and his buddies had watched, in which the "dogs" were students wearing only gym shorts and hiking boots as they trudged through the snow. He also remembered the ever-present mounds of snow and the old brick dorm building he had lived in. It looked like an old school building itself, with dormers projecting from its high, steeply sloped roof.

He nodded: Yes, he remembered his first year of college.

While Melissa talked to him, he realized he saw two of her. He saw two of everything he looked at. He squinted. Still two. He turned his head slightly, one way and then the other. That made him dizzy. The room spun even after he stopped turning his head. He felt like he had jumped off a building. His stomach was churning in his gut. He shut his eyes until he stabilized.

Melissa apparently noticed his head turns and said, "You have double vision. Things look kind of funny to you, don't they?"

"Funny?" he thought. "There's two of everything. The world is swimming around me; nothing stays still. There's nothing funny about it."

She said, "Your vision may return to normal in a week or two. Dr. Adler can tell you more about that. Can you raise your right hand?"

No, he couldn't. She wrote something on the form in front of her.

"Can you raise your left hand?" He raised it. She wrote something else.

In the course of the tests Melissa gave him, Jeremy also discovered that he couldn't move his right leg, he couldn't close his mouth or his right eye completely, and he had no feeling on the right side of his face.

Although he couldn't talk, sentences tumbled through his head. It seemed, now that he couldn't speak, he had more to say than he ever had in his life. And he was feeling things he'd never felt before, or that he hadn't felt since he was a child. He did feel like a child again: wide open, vulnerable, defenseless. He wanted someone to hold him closely and protect him, as if he had just awakened from a bad dream.

He noticed the way Melissa held her pen, the tightening of her jaw as she drummed the pen gently whenever she asked him a question, the way a little place on her temple vibrated when she brushed her dark brown hair aside to write something, as if there were a tiny heart underneath. When he looked at her darting eyes, he sensed her tension as if it originated from within him.

He wondered if he had a new sense, in addition to the five he'd had previously, that made him suddenly aware of emotions, both his and other people's. Indeed, he seemed to be at the mercy of emotions. He felt completely powerless against them. He had lost his former control over his feelings. Alternating sensations of fear and gratitude tumbled through his mind as quickly as his thoughts tumbled through his head. He flipped through emotions like they were cards in a deck. He was unaware of his body. The center of his thoughts and imaginings shifted back and forth between his aloneness and his perceptions of human kindness.

When Melissa sat in silence, writing, his thoughts would turn to dark fantasies of sinister doctors and abusive nurses, against whom he was defenseless. He feared the doctors would perform operations on him that would keep him unable to return to the outside world. He imagined the nurses would deprive him of proper nourishment and keep him subdued with tranquilizers. These thoughts created currents of silent unease in his mind and ripples of discomfort in his belly. But these feelings would instantly change to gentle washes of warm comfort as soon as Melissa uttered a few words of encouragement, or when she mentioned some familiar name or place from his past. As he looked at her, he remembered the pretty dark-haired girl in junior high. He had liked Sue but been afraid to speak to her. Was he getting a second chance now at all the relationships which he had been too afraid to pursue? Had he died, and was now reborn? Or was he still dead and having an out-of-body experience? Maybe he wasn't really here at all, in a physical sense, but was a soul floating above this ugly orange wheelchair, enclosed in this little windowless room. But how could he see, if he really had no body? And why couldn't he just fly off somewhere? Why was he stuck here above this chair? He looked down at the cracked orange vinyl covering the arms of his wheelchair. He wondered why he couldn't move his right arm or leg. He tried again. He could picture his right arm lifting, but it wouldn't move, as if it were someone else's arm. He couldn't even feel it.

He lifted his left arm, to make sure that that arm was still his. It lifted as soon as he thought about lifting it.

Melissa called him back to awareness of the outside world. "Do you know why you're here?"

He shook his head, unsure of what she meant by *here*. Was she talking about metaphysics, the old philosophical question of man's existence, or did she mean, "Why are you in this room answering questions?" He grinned as he thought of what his reply could have been if he could have spoken. He remembered the attitude toward life he had developed in the past year, his answer to all the degradation he'd quietly taken from kids when he was growing up. He wanted to say, "Fuck it. I don't need a purpose. I'm here, and I'm going to live life the way I want."

But his old life was lost in a dense fog. He had recognized the shapes and presences of his mother and father out in the lobby, but everything else he saw was unfamiliar and foreign, like the strange trees he had seen outside. It was as if he had been beamed to a different planet like a character on *Star Trek*.

Melissa explained what had happened to him at Cass Spars, how they thought the sailboat's mast had rolled off the supports and landed on his head. But even that was uncertain. No one had seen it. She told him the events, how he had been airlifted to Western Medical Center, spent several days in a coma, then began showing signs of awareness. Today, July 9, he had been transported to this hospital. It all sounded logical to Jeremy, as if she was describing the plot of a movie that he had seen once and then forgotten. He wasn't surprised to hear what had happened. Instead, he felt things fall into place, begin to make sense. He couldn't remember any of these things happening, his family's move to California or his work at Cass Spars, but it all seemed reasonable. It had the quiet certainty of deadly truth.

Out of the Fog

John Milam

Your vague shapes and centerless voices
circulate around me
as I sleepwalk the wet sand
in this dreary sea of mists.

I have wandered this empty beach for days
and weeks
amid your heavy sighs
and hopeful messages.
You radiate warmth and life,
huddling around my motionless body,
a remnant of the son and brother you knew
who, of course, could handle anything.

I want to reach out of the fog to you
but my arms won't obey.

Your voices lend me reality,
a firm dry rock I lean on
in this damp and desolate twilight,
wandering
the outer fringes of consciousness.

I'll be home soon.

John Milam

White Time

I take white time
and fold it in sections,
transfix reflections,
cut and paste
from scattered memories.
Glass-enclosed days form
onto vacant pages
that cover my winter-lighted desk.

The ground outside is as white
and barren
as airless light
cast from the sunlit moon.

But teenage friends crack jokes
as they crack open beers,
Mom and Dad argue over dinner
and call it discussion,
in-laws gossip under California sun,
and my nieces pout and holler
on the empty white pages.

John Milam

Signs and Sunflowers

1.
Whipping down Main Street the following spring,
a pale blue sign in front of a gas station advertises,
Automatic Self Serve.
It's the same shade of blue as her eyes,
I remember,
her eyes that pleaded with me to stay.
But you don't even have to talk these days,
just stick your plastic in, pump, and go.
Then a car the color of ketchup swings by me
with a mustard-yellow sign on its roof:
Call 1-800-STAY OUT!
for a sure-fire security system.

2.
I coast downhill on a late summer day,
fields and farmhouses parted by lines
of self-assured maples
that blow raucously in the strong wind
outside the capsule of my car.
Clouds billow on one side of the sky
in a purple-rimmed, sunlit, textured expanse,
holding all that's in heaven as I run out of town.
Another field approaches on my right,
and a thousand yellow winks cast out to me
from a thousand yellow eyes lying in the green:
Sunflowers, I think, smiling.
I know they winked at me
just before I looked straight into their eyes,
thinking,
Yes.

Retreat

The star below my window is a glimmer in the chrome of a parked truck on the dark street. I am blinking off my after-dinner doze, peering out of the venetian blind above my couch. I am sure those are her headlights cutting through the night air, reflecting up to me off the shiny metal. The star grows brighter and larger as she approaches. It isn't pure white, but shaded slightly toward yellow or orange.

The discolored dot of light is bright enough to ignite the air inside me. The atmosphere around me heats up. My eyebrows sweat. My stomach tightens. As the physical fact of her rolls into view, I see she's tucked behind the steering wheel in a sweet anxious bundle, a delicate creature running a large machine down a narrow street between towering houses.

Here and there, I notice reflections of other lights, winking their bright beings into and out of my nighttime world.

But she is returning. My stomach quivers, remembering. The scariest thing is always the simplest, the most painfully obvious. I needed her. Why couldn't I have just told her?

But the truth would launch me off a precipice, and I might just fall, uncaught. Like kids in childhood games, I could imagine her standing and laughing as I plummeted.

Or, after I'd been caught, I might roll over one night and find I'm pressing my nose to another wall. I might want to roll off the edge and begin free-falling again. After all, I've been falling free all my life. I'm used to it. The open air may be empty, but it makes a soft, forgiving bed. Home.

A bed in which I lie regretting every retreat, pounding my head against the wall of solitude that solidifies out of my open air. If someone would only open a door, the wall would fall around me, crumble like clumped sugar. I could get up and shake loneliness off for good and always.

The headlights disappear down the street. I sink back onto the couch and roll over, my face buried in the crook of my arm.

After the California Rains, January 1995

John Milam

Flying nowhere today,
held down by the concrete sky,
I drive through Oceanside after the storm
that washed Mom and Dad from their trailer.

Wind-torn palm branches lie in wet heaps
on the deserted street.
They still look green and alive
where they bleed like freshly killed animals.

I park by the pier,
wander the sediment and kelp
that now fill the parking lot.
I want to use the bathroom,
but it's flooded with soggy sand,
the door broken in by the weather.

I wander on—
fine grey mounds of sea-smelling silt
line the concession stand,
where crabs start tiny wet avalanches
as they dig out to the grainy light.

Looking up toward town,
my eyes can't even penetrate
the embankment's rain-carved cavern
that reaches under the stairway.

Maybe a giant tried to pick up the city
last night and, frustrated,
cast it back down on the seashore.

John Milam

Mercury

Our Selves
are like silver beads of mercury
on a black formica lab table.

Glistening,
we steal someone's attention from the teacher,
who fingers his mustache
and chalks another equation on the board.

Shimmering,
our perfection proves intangible
as we flee from the glare of scrutiny
or the press of a finger
into liquid metallic distortion,

again to collect in solitude.

The Hunt

Isaac's van had two small tinted rear windows, gun-racks mounted on the sides, and sand-colored insulating foam all over the walls and ceiling. He had told Jeremy the foam was to retain the heat for winter hunting, when he would use the van as a deer-blind. Sitting in the passenger seat, Jeremy felt like a cave was opening up behind him, and the uneven foam coating looked as if dripping water had created contours on the roof that would one day become stalactites, like teeth in the mouth of a great prehistoric beast.

Jeremy and Isaac were roommates and members of the Northwest Singles Group that meets near Detroit. Jeremy paged through one of the hunting magazines which were strewn about the van. He didn't care much about hunting, but he liked the outdoor scenes of rivers and forests and animals. The glare from the sun on the glossy pages hurt his eyes, so he reached down and groped through his pack for his sunglasses.

On this July Saturday morning, the Northwest Singles had reserved some canoes for a day trip on the Huron River. They would pick up the canoes at a livery near Wixom and paddle downriver to Milford.

Isaac continued his oratory, gently fingering his full shaggy mustache as if it were a sore on his upper lip. "But I think, sometimes, women don't communicate well either. I try to be honest, and people don't always like me for it. I guess they think I'm too honest. But if I'm going to get to know someone, and have her get to know me, I have to be honest. People tell me I say the wrong things sometimes, and I guess I do, but I'm just trying to relax and be spontaneous. People want you to be spontaneous, but they want you to say the right things, too."

"Yeah, I know that's true," Jeremy said. But he wasn't going to worry about that today. He'd been working six and seven days a week for the last two months, and he finally had a day to relax.

Isaac continued, "So I'm just going to have fun, and not worry so much about meeting women."

As they came to the Wixom exit, Jeremy read back the directions that Isaac had scrawled on a legal pad as the group leader described how to find the canoe livery. "Look for the big wooden sign on the left," he read. "Timothy's Bar & Grill. It's supposed to be back off the road a little."

When they found it, they parked in the gravel parking lot, amid dustclouds from other arriving cars, and walked over to where the rest of the group was meeting.

Two women Jeremy had met at a dance a few weeks ago, Michelle and Tracy, stood talking on the near side of the crowd. When he had first approached their table that night at the dance, they had smiled at each other. But after he had talked with them for a few minutes, they'd gone to the ladies room and he'd seen them come back to a different table. "But that was at night when I was tired," he thought. He knew he sounded bad when he was tired.

Instead of risking another rejection, he scanned the group for someone else to talk to. He saw a woman sitting in the sun, her legs crossed Indian-style, on the other side of the group. Her brown hair was swept across her forehead in a delicate wave that seemed to shield her eyes, and in back it fell freely. She sat a little apart from the group, but that didn't seem to bother her. She smiled at Jeremy when she saw him looking. He cut through the crowd, making his way to her, before he had a chance to become afraid.

"Hi," Jeremy started cheerfully, hoping to keep his pitch up to a normal level so he wouldn't sound half asleep. He had a slight speech impediment since a closed head injury ten years earlier, when he was eighteen. He looked the same as he always had, but when someone watched him closely, Jeremy noticed that he or she would often look at him strangely, as if he somehow stood out. He knew he did things a little more slowly than before. But he didn't think it was noticeable, until he became tired.

But today, preparing for a day of relaxation and fun, Jeremy was well-rested and energetic. He saw no reason to bring attention to his disability sooner than necessary.

"Hi," the brown-haired girl said, smiling back to him as she stood up. He guessed he must have sounded okay. "I'm Lisa."

"I'm Jeremy." He was determined not to freeze up and fall silent, having nothing to say. "Have you canoed before?" he asked her. It was the first thing he thought of to say.

"A little. I don't really know how," she said, still smiling.

"I learned how when I was a kid at camp," he said. "I think I can remember most of it. Do you want to ride with me?"

"Sure. I'm glad to find someone who knows what he's doing. The person in back steers, right?"

"Yeah. I'll take the back. Then it'll be my fault when we hit things."

She laughed. He liked her. She had a sense of humor.

"You can fend off the alligators," he said, turning to search the cattails and lily pads in the river for a pair of bulbous eyes. She laughed again.

Jeremy paddled hard as the group left the livery and entered the forest. He felt like they were going under the edge of a blanket. One by one, each person stopped paddling as he or she passed under the trees, as if the deepness of the forest demanded silence. Birds chirped in the trees above and frogs peeped from within the weeds on the muddy riverbanks. Bob, whom Jeremy knew from other events with the Northwest Singles, slapped his paddle down on the surface of the water, sending a jet of water onto the riverbank at the unprepared frogs. Michelle and Tracey shook their heads from the canoe behind. Bob chuckled.

They soon came to a break in the forest where lily pads formed a sunny carpet of pale green extending from the banks. Canadian geese flew in honking formation overhead, and tall, slender white birds stood along the banks like sentinels to monitor the passing caravan of canoes.

"Do you work?" Jeremy asked Lisa. He wanted to know more about her, and it was the first thing he thought of to say. Right after he said it, he wondered if it was the wrong thing to ask. She might think he was prying too much, or that he thought working was the most important thing a person did. He regretted it, wishing he could think of another way to open conversation. He thought of explaining it all to her right away: that many of the head injury survivors Jeremy knew weren't able to work, although most of them wanted to, and that for survivors of brain injury, working for a living becomes a privilege and a goal, not an obligation. But he hadn't even told her about his injury yet. She wouldn't know what he was talking about if he just launched into the subject. He'd made that mistake before.

Lisa partially turned her head around to eye him from the front seat of the canoe. Then her face relaxed again. Apparently she'd decided his question wasn't too outlandish. "Yes, I'm a physical therapist," she said.

Grateful for the point of familiarity, he said, "I worked with P.T.'s after I had a head injury. I had to learn to walk and use my right arm again."

"You had a head injury?" She sounded impressed, as if he'd just told her he'd climbed Mt. Everest last summer. "Were you in a coma?" This was a customary question among people familiar with head injury. The amount of time a person spends in a coma roughly determines how severe the effects of the injury on the brain will be, the residual effects, as Jeremy had learned from pamphlets in doctors' offices.

"For about a week," Jeremy said. Many survivors he knew had spent months in a coma, so he considered himself one of the lucky ones, as head injuries went. He was still able to do most of the things he could do before, although not quite as quickly or as gracefully.

"Wow," Lisa said. "You seem like you're doing great to me. I never would have known. You're really motivated, too. I can tell. Some of the people I work with could learn from you, people who haven't had as serious an injury as you've had." She hesitated, then asked, "How did it happen?"

"I was at work in Chicago, where I used to live, about ten years ago. A piece of steel swung into my head when they were moving it with a lift. I don't remember it, but that's how my dad told me it happened. He went back to visit the plant the next day. They told him I wasn't wearing a hard hat. Knowing myself before, I probably wasn't. That's the way I was. If someone told me to do something one way, I'd try to do it another way."

Lisa tried to lighten the conversation again. "I went to Chicago last December with some people from work. I remember walking with crowds of people through Marshall Field's and riding on the escalators. All over the store, they had ribbons and lights and plastic snowmen and elves." She laughed. "The pine boughs between the up and down escalators spilled off the partition whenever someone brushed against them. They had to keep stopping the escalator to pick up the branches so they wouldn't get pulled down through the grate at the end."

After they had canoed a while longer, Lisa said, "Some friends of my parents are having a party next weekend. It's not going to be wild or anything, just some people getting together and barbequeing. They do this a few times every summer, and they usually have a volleyball net."

He paused for a moment, unprepared. He realized she was asking him out, but he didn't know how to respond. His stomach leaped, and he felt like he had just jumped out of an airplane.

After regaining his breath, he managed to say, "That sounds fun. I like to play volleyball." He thought about the correct way to proceed from here. "Can I have your phone number?" he said.

"Well, I just met you."

Jeremy thought she sounded sorry that she had to be so cautious.

She continued, "Why don't you give me yours? I have some paper in my car. Don't let me forget."

Jeremy thought she sounded sincere. Maybe she really would call. Laughing, he said, "I'm head injured. I'll do my best to remember, but I can't promise anything."

After canoeing, the group waited by a bridge for the vans from the livery to pick them up. Jeremy guessed it was about ninety degrees by then. He and a few of the other men began jumping off the bridge into the river. Each one (except Jeremy) gave a high-pitched yell as he hit the water. As he watched, Jeremy strained his eyes to see through the muddy water to the bottom, so he could judge whether it was safe to jump. What if there was a rock down there? But it was like trying to see through chocolate milk. When two of the other guys executed their jumps safely, he followed. Lisa sat on the bridge's guard rail in the sun.

Soon the vans came, and everyone crowded into them to ride back to the livery where they had started. Lisa and Jeremy sat pressed side-by-side on the vinyl seat.

When they arrived at the livery, the group piled out of the van, like it was a freshly opened can of tamales.

"Hey, do you guys want to go have some dinner?" Jeremy heard from behind him. He turned to see Isaac, whom he'd temporarily forgotten. Isaac stood with Bob, Michelle, and Tracey. Jeremy turned to Lisa, who had also stopped to see where this invitation had originated. Lisa shrugged and said, "Sure, that sounds fun. Let me get my purse." She started towards a white Toyota pickup.

When she returned, the group of six went into the light brown wood-frame building that was Timothy's Bar & Grill. It looked too small to house a bar and restaurant, especially, Jeremy thought, one that could hold as many people as had parked their cars outside.

Jeremy was the first one to the entrance, a sliding glass door. He pulled on the handle to slide it across, but his fingers gave way, letting his hand fly empty across the space in front of him. Embarrassed, he reached up to try again. He realized how exhausted he was. Lisa said from behind him, "You're worn out, huh?" He looked at her. She smiled, and he tried to smile back as he gripped the handle tightly and pulled the door open.

When they got inside, the noise enveloped Jeremy like a coating of molten lead that threatened to seep into his ears. But he didn't want the day to end yet. He was determined to hold out, although he was craving peace and solitude to recuperate from the activity of the day. Bob and Isaac cracked jokes in the crowded bar as they waited for a table. Lisa, Tracy, and Michelle laughed politely. Jeremy remained quiet, drinking decaffeinated coffee while the rest of them drank wine or beer. After about fifteen minutes, a hostess showed them to a table.

After they ordered and their food arrived, Isaac and Bob both sent their dinners back. Isaac's ribs were too dry and Bob's steak was cold. Jeremy wondered if they were just trying to impress the women at the table. He and Lisa looked at each other with a knowing smirk.

Toward the end of dinner, Lisa noticed Jeremy was sitting quietly, not saying much.

"Are you okay?" she asked.

"Yeah, just tired," he said.

"You worked so hard canoeing."

"I guess I overdid it."

"You're in good shape," Lisa said, smiling discreetly and looking directly into his eyes. Jeremy felt a quivering excitement deep within him. For that one instant he felt connected with her on a primal level. Then it was over—not forgotten, but set aside for now. He knew they had shared a piece of their souls at that moment, a basic need for union that was beneath any words they could speak and any external details of ordinary life. He savored the unspoken intimacy.

Lisa broke the silence. "Yeah, I wish I could stay out all night like I used to in college, then go to classes and work the next day."

Jeremy wanted to say "No, that's not what I mean. It's not the same thing." But he realized they *were* talking about the same thing. Lisa had probably gone through changes in her life just as he had.

Jeremy was glad he'd met Lisa, but he knew from past experience not to let himself get excited too quickly. He had only just met her. The more fantasizing he had done in the past about a new girl, the more disappointed and depressed he'd become when things didn't work out as he'd imagined they would. So he reminded himself to just take things as they came.

Jeremy remained quiet through most of dinner. When he looked at Lisa, she smiled back to him. He imagined her saying, "It's okay."

After everyone said goodnight, Jeremy walked with Lisa to her truck.

"I had fun today," she said. "I'll find out what time that party starts next weekend."

"I'll give you my phone number," he said. "If I can find something to write it on." He searched through his wallet.

"You can write it on the back of this," she said, handing him a pen from her purse and the business card Bob gave to all the women he met. Jeremy had witnessed Bob's technique at the dances that the Northwest Singles held once a month. As soon as Bob met a woman, his hand dove into his back pocket and brought out his wallet, which flipped open to display several business cards waiting at his fingertips. He owned a plumbing service, and his card showed a man crouched down in front of a sink with his pants riding low in back. The caption read, *Crack service.* Jeremy laughed even though he had seen the card many times. He turned it over and wrote his name and number down.

He looked at Lisa again and said, "I'll talk to you soon."

"I'll call you," she said.

They both smiled as Jeremy turned toward Isaac's van. Isaac waited patiently at the wheel.

The next day, Sunday, Jeremy felt excited and still hopeful; he didn't expect her to call that soon.

Monday, after a day at work, he needed his spirits raised, so he hoped she would call that evening. As the hours and TV sitcoms went by, he began accepting that she had changed her mind about him, or that she was just being nice when she'd said she'd call.

When he got home from work Tuesday night, the answering machine flashed that there were two messages. He didn't play them back right away, but instead unloaded his lunch cooler of the empty plastic sandwich container and threw his wallet and pocket change on the dining room table next to his daily planner, checking to see if anything was up for tonight. Then he opened the windows to get some fresh air, walked calmly over to the answering machine, sat down on the couch, and pressed "play."

"Hey, Isaac, how's it going?" Jeremy held down the fast forward button to bypass his roommate's message and get to the next one.

"Hi, this is for Jeremy, from Lisa. We met on the canoe trip."

Bethany Schryburt
Exploring Senses

When I almost touch another woman or man with words that chill or bring on sensual heat, I feel life's celebration. My spirit bubbles with pleasure, to know I can draw laughter, or tears. Words can be powerful. I want to experience the kind of communication that knocks down walls and constructs bridges.

I pick up this razor-blade I call my pen and begin to slice through the surface, exploring my senses. Communication begins with a single word, *I*.

Bethany Schryburt

Skin to Skin

The Stimson Family Reunion came every year, like clockwork, on the first Sunday in August at the Lapeer County Park. It was a place where past met present. Wrinkly large aunts squeezed out my loving grunt, and lanky uncles with ticklish mustaches brought a rash to my cheeks. We joined around food, which was spread on four large, papered picnic tables, and I knew that every year Aunt Lottie's spicy apple pie and double-layered chocolate cake would look more inviting than Mom's potato salad and Aunt Margaret's deep-fried chicken. The endless minutes from the first *My how you've grown!* to the awaited *Let's eat!* were a little like waiting for the dentist to get his hand out of your mouth and offer you a cherry-flavored sucker.

If it wasn't for that spring water stream rambling between maple trees, just down the hill from the picnic tables, I would have been painfully bored.

"Hey, watch out where you're throwing those rocks," he yelled. The sun hit him square in the eyes as he looked up at me. I squatted on the bank, my dark hair covering my hazel gold eyes. After that rock splashed, I picked up another one and held it tight in my fist.

"Sorry, I didn't see you," I quickly replied. "I was aiming for that big green bull frog, over near that tree limb in front of you."

"Why?" My cousin David's skinny body balanced on a fallen tree stretched out over the water. His face was covered with freckles and his sandy brown hair stood straight up from the top of his head, leaving nothing to hide his ears, which tilted out, like the wings of a butterfly. When I didn't answer him fast enough, he splashed a handful of water at me and yelled, "Hey you! Why?"

I plopped my rear end on the wet grass and tried to decide if I could trust him with the truth. "Cause if I knock 'em just right, he'll turn belly up and then I can snatch him up out of the water and feel his skin," I said.

He started to smile. "Is that all you ever do, just feel 'em and throw 'em back?"

I slid down the bank and let my bare feet ooze through the murky bottom to the tree where he stood. Then I jumped up and stood on the tree, looking right into his dark brown eyes. "Once I cut one open." I released eye contact. "But you only have to do that once," I whispered. "Anymore, and it's just being mean."

"Yeah, you're right." He slipped his hands in his pockets and smiled. "Maybe your mom and dad would let you stay at my place a couple of nights." Then he added. "I've got charts at my house that show all the details of a frog's insides."

We spent more than two hours just knocking frogs out cold and picking them up. Then we ran our fingers over their backs and stomachs and sometimes pushed a little harder to imagine where all the stuff was located in them.

That night I went home with David for a two-day adventure that made me want to be a scientist. In his bedroom, there were picture books about reptiles, rocks, stars, and fish. The room was jammed floor to ceiling with microscopes, skeleton models, bug collections, telescopes, moon charts, butterfly nets, taxidermy projects, specimen jars, and the stuffy smell of formaldehyde mixed with rotting moths.

The following week, David spent with me, on my turf. The first place we went was a stagnant pond, where we dug for salamanders—florescent orange, nearly sightless. We collected six and found them a new home—my basement, where we stored wood for our furnace. The rotting wood gave them a cool, damp place to snuggle.

Tuesday morning, we sat on the steps of the front porch, trying to decide what to do. "Do you wanna build a fort in the barn, or fix up my tree house behind the garden?" I looked at his face, trying to see a sign, but he just looked up at a daddy-long-legs spider, walking down the side of the house. "Hey, David, which do you wanna do?"

"Let's fix-up the tree house and then maybe your mom will let us sleep in it on Friday night." The words rushed out of his mouth like flies out of the barn. Then he jumped to his feet and turned to look down at me. "Where do we start?"

First, we repaired broken boards and loose nails. Next, we trimmed branches to make an opening for the telescope. David and I worked all day, marking off rooms and designing a rope pulley system to haul boards, chairs, and tables up to the platform, which was securely balanced between the two main branches of the apple tree. By late afternoon, our dirty sweat-streaked faces made us look like Indians preparing for war. We had fun spraying the dirt off each other with the garden hose.

On Wednesday, we lay side by side in the tall warm grass, silently waiting. I whispered in a hoarse voice. "David, get ready. I can feel the pounding of little feet." Suddenly, a rabbit ran through the meadow of wild mustard and onto our trail. David lifted my .22 rifle and fired a single shot, killing the rabbit. It dropped and we stood over it, expecting something.

"Good shot, David!" As I picked up the still-warm rabbit, slinging it around my neck, I gazed admiringly at a would-be-Davy Crocket. "I'll show you how I skin these kind of critters, and then my mom will cook it for supper."

On Thursday we had to work in the garden, picking tomato worms off the stems of the strong-smelling succulent plants. I had an idea. "David, let's use a knife and peel the skins away." The worms wiggled, but David and I were able to dissect them, gently lifting the concealing tissue from the grub-like bodies.

David brought his nose down real close to the cutting board, then he twisted around to look at me. "Gosh, Beth, I can't even tell if they're male or female." We both started laughing. "I guess it don't much matter. Hey, maybe they're like earthworms and have both sexes in the same body."

"Grab that board over there, David, and we'll tack them up with these straight pins." While we stretched out the sticky skins, I kept my eyes fixed on the board. "Maybe when the skin dries, we can put it under the microscope."

Because it was raining, our plans to hike to Hassler Lake on Friday went down the drain. We ran to the barn and made tunnels in the bales of hay. We were deep inside a tunnel, breathing in the clover sweetness. It was close. Our arms were touching, skin to skin. Then, like a couple of groundhogs, we popped our heads up into the stream of light filled with hay dust. "Follow me, David, and I'll show you my world from the top."

We climbed the ladder at the end of the barn, where I pointed to baby pigeons in their nest, three feet from the window. Their scrawny bodies pulsed and their beaks, too big for their heads, remained open waiting for worms. High up near the top of the barn, with the rain hitting the tin roof, it sounded like an Indian chant, encouraging a sun dance.

This was the night we spent in the apple tree, gazing at the Milky Way, the North Star, and the moon through David's telescope. While we munched on popcorn and apples, David pointed out constellations. "O.K., you see where that bright North Star is?" He looked intently into the heavens and then looked back at me. "Well, when you follow it out, you'll find the Big Dipper."

"You know a lot about book science, David, but I like to feel it, touch it, and smell it before I know it." Somewhere in the back of my mind, I was determined to get to know a lot more about David, in the same way I knew about everything that surrounded me in my world.

I leaned my head back on the scratchy bark of the apple tree, not knowing how to bring up my idea. "David, I was reading *The Autobiography of Benjamin Franklin,* and he enjoyed taking air baths."

David propped himself up on one elbow. "What d'ya mean, air baths?"

"Near as I can tell, old Ben liked to feel the breeze on his bare skin, all of it." I sat up. "Sometimes clothes get in the way of feeling, ya know?" Then I softly continued. "Have you ever wondered what it'd be like to be naked in the night air?"

Neither of us spoke for a long time, and then David rolled over on his belly. "D'ya mean, kinda like a science experiment?" Then he got a real serious look on his face. "Are you sure, Beth?" David asked with a wild kind of look in his eyes.

When I nodded yes, we each took off one item at a time, slowly tucking them inside the sleeping bags. "This'll have to be a secret, and we'll keep the sleeping bags close by, just in case someone comes out here."

I looked over all of David's body. His maleness didn't surprise me, because I had seen lots of farm animals, but his skin looked kind of see-through with the light from the full moon behind him. He kind of looked beautiful, like that picture of a statue of David that I remembered seeing in the art books at school.

We dropped down onto the sleeping bags, stretching our bodies out straight with our skin almost touching. The cool August breeze caressed every crack and fold of my skin. His downy body hair stood at attention with the coolness of the night air, and my skin worked at producing goose-bumps.

I lifted my left hand. "David, let's make a special ceremony."

David raised his right hand, then gently our pinkie fingers locked together. I touched him with my right hand and pressed here and there, trying to understand what was under his skin. He answered back with presses of his own.

Then we sat up and folded our legs Indian style. "Beth, I got an idea." He squinted, trying to see my eyes better. "If we prick our fingers and join them together, we'll become blood brothers, like Tom Sawyer and Huckleberry Finn." We sat on the edge of the platform, and David found his pocket knife. After he pushed the point of the blade into his index finger, I took the knife and did the same to mine. We both squeezed our fingers until a glistening trickle of blood ran out. We pressed them together hard.

I saw David the next summer at the Stimson Reunion. He was standing near the water fountain, with his skinny arms folded at his chest. I glanced up at him and then noticed his eyes fixed on my pre-teen nipples, like two fried eggs, sunny-side-up, under my shirt. My cheeks became flushed, and I quickly bent to get a mouthful of water. David kicked at a stone and scratched the back of his head. One of the cousins was calling him to join in the baseball game. At the same time, my mother was calling for me to come help her empty the picnic basket.

I cleared my throat. "So, did you have a good year at school?"

David looked over my head towards the ball diamond and mumbled his answer. "Yeah, it was all right." He was careful not to look into my eyes. "See ya around." He ran away, like the devil was behind him.

Bethany Schryburt

Bovine Baptist

I peek down a trap door
at my brother, Paul,
five years older, ten years wiser.
He wants to preach. At
thirteen, he knows the Lord.
On a three-legged-stool
Paul raises his hands
over black and white cows.
Spider webs drape in clumps from
hand-planed rafters,
dingy with dust. Holstein
parishioners held captive
by his gaze, moo in recognition.

Hell-fire and brimstone to those
who will not repent! Paul shakes
The Bible in the air and brings
it down with a *whack* on his thigh.
A bantam rooster crows, and three
Berkshire pigs oink in harmony.

I stretch out across a bale of hay.
Prince, my dog, dreams at my feet.
I hear laws straight from Leviticus,
and the poetry of King David.
Rock of Ages quakes basement windows.
Collection begins, one squirt at a time,
white streams in a silver pail.

Bethany Schryburt

Grandma Jessie

I bite into an open-faced sandwich,
cut into four, slathered with butter
and topped off with strawberry jam.
I nibble the edge and tip it just so,
watch a red stream of goo
meander down a skinny wrist.
I lick it, just before the elbow.

Hollyhocks in delicate pinks and yellows
lean against a dirty white clap-board.
Peonies, platter-size, blood red or pinkish white
fill the air with sweetness beyond belief,
as millions of black ants suck-up nectar.
My nose nestles close to the ground
to breathe pungent Lilly-of-the-Valley,
while purple violets tickle my toes.

Black patent leather shoes
with thick heels and strong laces
shuffle on wooden floors. Her
black cane, rubbed smooth at the handle,
a rubber tip on the end, taps rhythmically.
I strain to hear her lack of sound, when
her finger gently touches her lower lip, pondering.
Her pencil hovers over a crossword puzzle.
The right word finds the tip of her tongue, and
she carefully fills in the squares.

Finding Clover Bottom

Annie Mae ran down the street, her heart thumping like a rabbit chased by a hound dog. She couldn't stand it anymore. Hazel Park was noisy with cars zooming past her and trucks honking for her to get out of the way. Annie Mae's feet hit the pavement solid and hard, then she turned left down the hill. She slid on the damp grass, landing on her bottom, next to the creek. Annie Mae's dark shaggy hair fell loose and covered her freckled face, hiding the tears that were making tracks along her cheek and neck. She crawled under the bridge. Then, she leaned against the cool wall. "Dad-burned school. They's the ones that's stupid. I ain't goen back, never."

Annie Mae and her family had to move to Hazel Park so her daddy could find work in some Detroit factory. She missed her country, Kentucky. Clover Bottom is her home. It's where she belongs. If only she could find a place in this cement world that could be as peaceful as Clover Bottom.

Annie Mae threw her shoes at the bridge's wall and, scooting closer to the creek bank, she stuck her toes in the cool water. "Damn," she yelled, and her voice echoed off the cement, shouting back at her. "It ain't fair." She hung her head and muttered, "I allus did what the Good Book said. Why is God letten me suffer?"

The air grew silent, and Annie Mae picked up a smooth stone, skipped it across the sparkling water. Ripples circled out from the center spots, as the stone bounced on the surface, reminding her of Mamaw.

When she closed her eyes, she felt herself wrapped in Mamaw's arms, being rocked in that creaking chair on the front stoop. Annie Mae could hear Mamaw's voice sweetly singing Irish Folksongs.

Annie began to sing and then looked intently near the water's edge, connecting with the eyes of a critter. She whispered to the large bull-frog, hiding in some green weeds, "I wanna go home."

Annie Mae stretched her lanky arms and stood on the soft muddy bank. As the brownish sand squished between her toes, she suddenly thought about going fishing in Red Lick, just north of Kerby Knob, where Mamaw's kin lived. It was the smell of earthy bait worms and the trout's glistening shimmer that flickered past her brain. "I ain't never gonna find Clover Bottom in this place." She hung her head and kicked at a rusty Spam can as she reached for her shoes.

As she slowly criss-crossed the vacant lots, she thought about how hard her ma had to work, taking care of things at Auntie Maude's and Uncle Will's place. Her cousins, Grover and Zack, didn't lift a finger around the house. Auntie Maude worked at the restaurant seven days-a-week, so she couldn't be expected to do house work. Uncle Will and her daddy worked at the Ford factory. Annie Mae was the oldest, and she did her best to help Ma with her little brother, Andrew, and baby sister, Emma, and also the twins, Noah and Ned. Somedays she dreamed about being rich like that girl at school, Jennifer Craig. But that was just a dream, like finding Clover Bottom.

Uncle Will and her cousin, Grover, were stretched out on the steps when Annie Mae walked across the grass to the front stoop. Uncle Will reached down and tousled her hair. "You're growin like a bad weed. I figger you're gonna be as big as Grover, afore long."

Annie Mae pulled open the screen door, letting it slam behind her, tight against her heels. "Ma, I'm home. You needin some help?"

Within an hour, everybody was gathering at the big kitchen table. The smell of fried chicken, biscuits and gravy filled the air. Annie knew there was banana pudding for dessert, so she'd even eat some of those turnip greens. Ma was getting ready to say the grace, because nobody could touch a fork until God was properly thanked. Ma's eyes glanced around the table, settling on Andrew. "Andrew Young, I recken you oughta go to that sink there and find you some soap and water." Andrew shyly slid off his chair and pulled it up to the sink.

Grace was said. Once everyone started eating, Ma looked over at Annie Mae.

"Mrs. Johnson called me today. She said you ain't been in school much this week. She said you left early today, and she wanted to be sure I knew about the picnic tomorrow."

Annie Mae looked down at her mashed potatoes. "I ain't goen back to that stupid school. I ain't."

Her daddy stopped buttering his biscuit, and laid his knife on his plate. He folded his hands under his chin. "Why ain't you goen back, Annie Mae?"

"They all hate me, even Mrs. Johnson." Annie Mae's voice trailed off, and her fingers dug into her knees. "They call me a dirty hillbilly."

Everyone started talking at the same time, telling about how she was right or how she should call those kids names back. Cousin Zack's voice shouted above the others. "Yu jist got to learn how to fit-in." He put his arm around Annie Mae and whispered in her ear. "I don't tell nobody that my name's Zechariah. They'd laugh their fool selves sick."

Later that night, propped up in her bed, Annie gazed at the dark cast iron treadle of the sewing machine against the far wall. In the middle of its curling iron-work, the word CONQUEST stood out, like an omen. Annie could feel the pride of her ancestors rising up in her chest. She knew she could learn the rules, could adjust. She had her family.

Just then Ma came in the room, carrying a patchwork quilt. "I thought you might wanta sleep under Mamaw's quilt tonight." Ma leaned down, kissing Annie Mae on the cheek, while sweeping back her unruly hair.

Annie Mae's eyes followed the uneven stitching around each quilt square, remembering every dress and shirt that found its way into Mamaw's quilt. It was the perfect charm to sleep under with the school picnic tomorrow. She would draw strength from Mamaw's memories. "I recken mebbe I'm a goen to the picnic tomorrow, Ma."

Sunshine peeked in Annie Mae's window, alerting her to the smells of breakfast and the sound of Noah and Ned running through the kitchen after Auntie Maude's tiger gray cat, Smoky. Annie Mae dressed in a flurry, careful to choose her best-looking shirt. When Annie Mae arrived in the kitchen, she realized how late she had slept in. Daddy and Uncle Will had already left for the factory, and Andrew was dressed and waiting on the stoop.

"Mornin, Annie Mae, ain't you the sleepy head?" Ma pulled out a chair and pointed to the bowl on the table. "Ya got ta eat some warm oatmeal. It'll stick ta yore ribs til the sun is a little warmer."

Annie Mae started to tell her ma that she couldn't eat a thing, but baby Emma started crying, sending Ma running to her bedroom and leaving Annie Mae alone. She spooned the steamy oatmeal into her mouth, rolling the black juicy raisins around with her tongue.

She was going to need all the energy she could get to face the school picnic at Jefferson Beach.

Annie Mae was carrying a paper sack containing a jelly sandwich that Ma had made for her and a little bag of New Era potato chips that Zack had given her for a special treat. Near the school's front door, she could see the new girl, Sally Bird, from Chicago. She was real pretty. Sally's long blond hair sparkled in the morning sunshine, like a fresh spring rain sparkles on a mountain top, and she had a red ribbon which pulled all her hair up into a dancing ponytail. Annie Mae whispered under her breath what Mamaw always used to tell her, "Yu ain't no better than nobody else and yu ain't no worse, so hold yore head up high." Annie Mae ran towards the school yelling, "Sally, Sally Bird, Sally."

Before Annie Mae could yell "hello," she went flying through the air, due to Billy Monroe's foot suddenly coming in front of her ankles. Billy grabbed her lunch and stuck his greasy head deep inside the bag. Annie Mae saw red. Her Irish temper flared, and she went at Billy like all hell broken loose, arms swinging, fists clenched. "Don't cha tech my poke. It's my poke, so get yore durn fool head outa it."

Billy Monroe was frightened. He looked around to see if anyone was watching, then he started yelling, "Help. Help. Somebody get this wild and crazy hillbilly away from me. Help. Help."

Mrs. Johnson ran around from behind the second bus, calling, "Annie Mae Young. Annie Mae. What are you doing?" Mrs. Johnson pulled Annie Mae away from Billy, who by now had a bloody nose. "Miss Young, you will sit in the front seat by yourself. You need to start thinking about how a young lady must act in the city."

Annie Mae didn't feel much like going on a picnic. She opened her bag. Ma's jelly sandwich looked flatter than a pancake, and the New Era potato chips were gone. Annie Mae lifted her head and looked around. She could see several willow trees over the hill behind the buses. All the kids were running towards the rides. Annie Mae didn't feel like riding a stupid miniature train or a silly merry-go-round. Defiantly, she marched towards the willow trees, the river bank, and solitude.

Along the trail, Annie Mae found pleasure in the brightness of the wild spring flowers: blue chicory, yellow goats-beard, delicate ladies-slipper, and even the plentiful dandelion brought a smile to her face. She headed down to the water's edge, thinking some fish might come close for pieces of her squashed jelly sandwich.

The peaceful silence was broken by some human sobs coming from behind the hemlock tree. Before she got completely around the tree, Annie Mae recognized the beautiful blond hair and the bright red ribbon. "Sally, what's wrong?" Annie Mae dropped her paper bag and kneeled beside Sally, looking into the red swollen eyes.

At first, Sally couldn't stop sobbing long enough to answer Annie Mae, but only managed to shake her head back and forth in a forlorn fashion. "I'm dying."

"Yore dyin?" Annie Mae glanced all over Sally for some sign of a wound or illness. "How'd ya know it. That yore dyin, I mean."

Sally twisted a piece of her dress into a tight knot and began to moan. "I was all right this morning. I mean, I felt a little funny inside, but I thought it was because of the picnic. You know?"

"So, what happened?" puzzled Annie Mae.

Sally whispered. "On the bus ride, I don't know. Maybe we hit a bump real hard or something," Sally hung her head, "or maybe I have been touching places at night that I should stay away from and God's punishing me." Sally began to cry again.

"Oh, for Pete's sake. Why don't yu jist tell me what's wrong?"

Sally turned her face away. "I have blood between my legs, and more is coming."

"Shoot. Yore not dyin. It's natural. It jist means yore becomin a woman." Annie shook her head in disbelief. "Didn't yore mama tell yu this would happen?"

Sally began crying again in deep rhythmic sobs. "It's just me and my dad. My mom died more than a year ago in a car accident."

Annie Mae reached around Sally's delicate body, giving her a warm hug. "Mamaw was right; we ain't no better nor worse than anybody." Annie Mae jumped up and headed for the bullrushes at the bottom of the hill. "I'm gonna git ya some cattail fluff to put in your pants. It'll feel jist fine, and it won't let the mess get on your pretty dress."

For once, Sally looked closely at this hillbilly girl. She wasn't so stupid. "Annie Mae, I think we're going to be real good friends for a long time."

As Annie Mae searched in the bullrushes for the best cattail tops, she thought about being needed and loved, and how both made a person feel warm inside—just like home, just like Clover Bottom.

Bethany Schryburt

Life Line

They sit close at the kitchen table.
He's defensive and distant, elbows on oak.
She's leaning into his body, skin on skin.
Time ticks urgency, an impartial face on
a papered wall. He sees its hands point at details.
She feels a new life stirring within her.

Silence tightens the air, and the clock
is a circle of repetition.

He remembers his insistent need.
She remembers her passionate heat.
He thinks about lost money, time, freedom.
She thinks about a heart, beating good-bye.

He works at a problem to be solved.
She plays with emotions unborn.
Tears begin to trickle down her cheek.

In frustrated anger he turns away.
          It's not that big a deal!
She pulls away in guilt.
          It's not your body.
          It's not your problem.

Bethany Schryburt

Pass It On

Violence grows in circles,
angry words, hateful looks.
Rough hands strike tender cheeks.
Pass it on.
Her mother crawls to the mattress edge.
Her father spits harsh words,
stones from a sling-shot.
Lazy Bitch. Ugly Whore.
Anger fills her house
with silent screams.
Pass it on.

Morning smells fill the air,
strong coffee, burning toast.
Her heartbeat echoes loud as
Mother finds spilt milk.
Fists fly out, punching skin.
Clumsy Kid. Stupid Child.

Her Teddy snuggles close.
She pulls his furry arm.
She throws him hard against the wall.
Stop Crying. Stupid Bear.
Wet fury flows into
a Mickey Mouse pillow.
Pass it on.

Bethany Schryburt

Try to Show You Like Her as Much as You Say You Love Her

You don't understand.
He quietly replied.
I pay attention to details,
things that are broken.
I don't need to praise what
suits me just fine.

You see, he sighed.
Just like my car,
it serves me well
and if it's broken,
then, I spend effort to fix it,
but I don't kiss it
just cause it runs.

Bethany Schryburt

Let It Rise

I watch bread rise.
Thoughts turn to a teenage son.
Puffed-up with ego, invincible,
he pushes past his limits.

With a thump to the middle
a triumphant loaf loses its air.

I knead the bread.
I miss my son.

Bittersweet bite of fennel
mixes with the heady aroma of yeast.
Boy Scouts, bike trips, saxophone,
football, senior prom, Oakland U.

At the back of a warm stove-top,
fragrant and active, under a kitchen towel,
manna from God, it pushes heavenward.

Out of sight, out of touch, time slowly ticks.
The bell rings, hot air blasts from an open door.
Crusty and warm, sweet butter melts.
His warmth reaches me.

Bethany Schryburt

Walnut Row Farm

A hint of fall chills the air.
Breath steams. Arm hairs rise.
My ears ring with staccato cricket cadence.
In grass they hide, wet with evening dew.

Muscles throb. Bones ache.
Still I try to keep up with Dad's hay baler.
Bend and lift, bend and lift, bend and lift.
Bales surge out of a cavernous combine,
relentless, monotonous, mechanical.

Abrasive weeds mix with clover. Bare skin scratches.
Dusty chaff finds its way under my clothes.
Salty sweat curves around eyebrows,
seeps in at thin lash edges, stings my eyes.

I lift my sleeve to my nose. I blow
hard, like Dad. I almost relax.
I can breathe, but the dark scares me.
I wonder, *How deep, how deep does the blackness go?*

From baler, to ground, to wagon, to barn,
Time stretches.
Dad and I find a soft spot in long grass.
Coolness welcomes us.
We lean our backs on a faded red door.
Ten inch wheels hang on a rusty track.
Paint fades, like history, around us.
Without looking—I see behind me,
just under the roof, white letters, two feet tall:
Walnut Row Farm, Stimson and Sons.

We chew on sweet alfalfa.
Silence enfolds us.
There's the Big Dipper.
I feel insignificant. I feel loved.

Bethany Schryburt

Naptime

Mother draws me in
to read a fairy tale,
my afternoon interruption
from sandbox towns and
butterfly hunts.

Sleeping Beauty reclines
in a glass casket silence.
The prince rides with sword
at his side, strong hero in metal.
Tales wind round hugs.
Rapunzel releases long
ladder-like hair. She's
used by the knight to climb
to the top of his kingdom.

A sleepy cadence hypnotizes me.
Before long, her words trail off,
and Mom's head nods. The paper
fantasy falls to the floor. Mom
snores on Grandma's quilt.

Paper heroes are male.
Paper maidens are fair.

I escape through the garden,
tumble down a grassy slope.
I rule my queendom,
not a cage made of glass,
not a tower without doors.

Mike Jones
The Patter of Bare Feet

Forget the Internet

Get unplugged, Jump-off, Nix the nebulous
incredulous web. You won't find me dancing
on that low wire act, another lone satellite
going nowhere in darkness
                              yet, thinking
about feelings that ride quick bursts, shocks
sent far without inflection, a wink, or tears.

Let's have some face here . . . Humanity
a flowing voice, etchings, a firm clap of hands
familiar looks — ancient, iconic, wonderful. . .

Before monitors, cables and modems — we met
evenings in parlors, on porches, park benches
over coffee and drinks, or smokes. We filled
our ears with sighs and laughter
                              found harmony
below the knees, in the supple arc of calves
a gentle turn of ankle and the patter of bare feet.

Mike Jones

Mad Science

"Personality Clue: Scientists find genetic explanation . . . "
"Detroit Free Press," January 2, 1996

They isolated my favorite gene, a variant—
a phone for chemicals with an extra long cord.

It regulates brain response to dopamine:
Strongly linked to pleasure and sensation . . .

The gene preferred most by 4 out of 5 poets.
The extravagant one that lavishes flowers

for no apparent reason. The impulsive gene
that stops at garage sales and blows nine bucks

on broken chairs, used books, and empty jars.
My New Year's Eve bash, lamp-shade, gene.

The gene that talked me into marriage
kids, a cat, finches and self-employment.

It's my fast driving, politically incorrect, gene.
My parents hated this gene when I was sixteen—

my tell-it-like-it-is, stand-up comic, I've had it
with you and your little dog too, gene.

The sensibility you get when you cross a desert
ram with a bat, and a goofy Neanderthal man.

Discovering Two New Planets

My son is afraid
aliens are going to get us for sure
now that we've seen
their watery planets floating
in the deepening heavens
through the Hubbell's diamond eye
sailing across the Milky Way
from Mission Control: Houston, Texas.
He says they might be bat-creatures
flapping earthward . . . Right now!
And we can't see their darkness
against a whole universe of night.
I tell him not to worry.
Flying is the strictest art
God's second greatest gift.
They're probably swimming
with plankton and whales. But, first
archipelagoes will appear
from beneath the ocean, volcanoes
erupt into mountain tops. Islets
then corals, seaweed and sunflower
trees spreading up, out toward their sun
thirty-five brief light-years from here—
I tell him as if the sky were falling—
wonderful things will learn to walk
by themselves soon, crawling awkward
onto barren rocks, or into tide pools
swirling like creations' soup
perfecting the future landscape.
The only thing to fear is—
I tell him in his universe—
the stranger to earthly desire.

Mike Jones

Bang Theory Revisited

Certainly there must be a chef.
Quantum physics dictates
the universe is a souffle continuously rising
five billion years after something snapped
or banged open like an oven door.

The proprietor demands order, always
attends to mundane daily details — dust,
sweep the grounds, clean the windows,
mop the bathroom tile with bleach,
and balance the books each night.

Gravity came first at 10 to the minus 43rd
of a second, a milli-fraction of a snap,
when pure energy split, positive-negative.
Then came hydrogen and helium— first
angels (forged from that infernal bang)
which roam in hot darkness then cool
into intensest suns.

Or, time— an invisible vine
weaving through the Brazilian rain forest.
And we, exotic flowers, sprawl
between tree limbs— as memory climbs
toward that green canopy
and topples across mossy branches
a million faint echoes whispering *bang*.

Epididymus

And I have dreamt the dream-snake dream.
It haunts me always, shadowing and lying
in ambush beneath my bedroom window
waiting for my first gentle snore—or sleep
shudder, that convulsion where one hand
clenching perception's vine releases *what is*
as the other grasps the tree of *what could* . . .
The snake bobs and slithers out-of-reach
toothlessly tonguing some lost secret,
more bassett hound than viper, almost comic
yet sad for forgetting all but that warm need.
I must shimmy down the tree, disregarding
how the bark and limbs cut my smooth,
unprotected, dream flesh, and slump into
the hollow where old roots pull at dark earth
until I fill that damp place, and welcome
the snake now working slowly up my legs—
peacefully offering its cold, scaly self up to
the vague knowledge of a coiled otherness
it's warmth descending.

Original Oil

The wicker basket slightly tipped,
one peach leans into ambient light
spilling from some unseen window
onto that dark table, polished clean.
The face of creation is an open flower
poised on that wiry, fruit bearing bough—
focus of seasons, almost conscious
of another, the movement and music.
It is the event of a singular division
precariously rippling with possibility,
then dryly plucked and haply settled
in the autumnal fullness of nature's art,
in the thinning scent of ripened peach,
two leaves, a stem, wet oils and canvas.

Mike Jones

Stitches for Baby Kate

Between the eyes, a thin line of blood
then red drops and streams.
The emergency room smells like tears.

It's an accident. She fell. The door jamb—
Falling did it. Lost her balance. It could . . .
The hinge—sideways—she fell—the falling.

Kate, which snowman has the purple scarf?
How many is two? Kate are you feeling . . .
She speaks very well for a two-year-old.

Is there a resident specialist, a plastic . . .
on call? Only for torn ears and eyelids.
Everyone recommended . . . Dr. Allen says . . .

Hold her head, hold her head still, hold . . .
My baby, it's O.K. we're going home soon
Daddy's here, it's O.K., almost done, it's . . .

No scarring, four small sutures tight as . . .
A pack of No. 7 strung to a fishbone needle
. . . like sewing memory without a scar.

Mike Jones

Thanksgiving Parade

The trickle begins on Main Street, our
families come together like marching bands

balloons and floats jockey for position.

I like a full house on the holidays, kisses
and madness, in-laws and out-laws, kids

drift across rooms like blown snow or leaves.

Or, from the kitchen to TV room to the bar
we flap and strut, bats and peacocks, each

with colorful, oversized paper-mache heads.

Nearly transparent paper-flower clothes
cover wood and wire frames, our designs

intent on pleasing and entertaining. Each

embellishes holiday memories of lost relatives
odd traditions, wild dishes, Thanksgiving—

parades of flowers and the virtue of crazy glue.

Power of Three

Be careful for what you wish . . . Magic powers
deceive the eye, the mind, the vested heart

with snowy doves, hats and rabbits— disappearance.

So, I asked for the trip of a lifetime and she
she misunderstood, distracted by that golden ring

then our whispered wish for something more.

Three balls makes for a good juggling act
one coming, one going, one winking-eye

level between life's wonder and weight. Hands

rough palms, face up search for warmth and light
as the reader passively gazes down, down and rubs

meaning into each fractured line, each life-scar

honed like the Grand Canyon by slow water—
sweat, tears, and spit: our earned inheritance.

You may just get it, and swing with the dynamic

of three— Or, one, two, three, five, eight leaves
in three turns of a daisy's stem. How snail shells

and generations of rabbits appear mathematically,

evolve like love's vows, juggling balls, doves . . .
a wish for something more . . . for deep water.

Mike Jones

The Gift and the Race

Things people have given me, or I myself, at times.
Some in boxes still, others used and discarded, still

others well-kept as treasures, preserved in my den.
They hang upon the walls: a sword from Paris

I won, bartering in broken French for half an hour,
a portrait, oil on board, of an immigrant child;

frayed jacket and olive cap, *The American Gazette*
tucked firmly beneath his left arm, right hand

raised to his lips, dark eyes that follow relentlessly.
Some awards, old photos, certificates and trophies.

But, all you ask is, *What's in the closet over there?*
That is my closet. I painted those doors chestnut brown

like the antique paneled walls Dr. Zubnikowski
brought here from his home on Edison, in Detroit,

and had reinstalled in what was to become my den
in my dream house, on Bloomcrest Drive near Troy.

What's in the closet in the corner? you ask again.
I even painted the hardware, so it would fade into

the wall, the way the banks of bookshelves wrap
around the room until they become book wallpaper

and begin to repeat themselves: *Great Expectations;*
Moby Dick; Hamlet; Inferno; The Aeneid and *The Odyssey.*

You tell me there is a lion in my closet. Yes, there is
the skin of a lion in my closet. The lion, gone into legend

as legend has it, a god among lions and great of heart, one
day came upon a goddess as a waterfall that leaps uphill,

and at her feet lay a pool of clear water, still and deep
as night. The lion saw in the water her image and his

reflected in that deep mountain pool, which is great like
the night, and his greatness raged to be with her water.

The lion roared until the mountain shook. Then his skin
fell-off, like a snake's. No, that's not it exactly. His skin

and his mane and claws, like a womb great with child,
pushed the lion's inner-greatness out through his mouth.

And the mountain shakes; the ground is slick with sacrifice:
the blood, tears, sweat and spit of greatness born.

But, the wind burns; the sky burns; and the ground pricks
the thing new born which is less like a lion, and not a man—

although it drags itself now, like a man, into the deep water
and disappears into darkness, as if a cave on the mountain,

and leaves in the light by the shore the skin and the waterfall.
His skin, too, is a gift: the experience and reminder of a race

that is run, and run, and run again. NOTE: The timid never
start the race. The weak die along the way. Those that fall and

raise themselves up, out of the mud and sweat and blood and
finish the race, earn the gift of shaggy hair and gilded claws.

Gravemaking

I.
No machine, no icon, no other hands
can do this. I must dig my own grave.
I reach for the best shovel I can find.
I scour hardware stores and lumber yards
appraising the character of shovels
and spades, picks and pick-axes—
their painted handles, polished steel
fittings and finish, weight and measure.
None is good enough. None will do.
Their handles hastily milled offshore.
Blades, fittings and metal shafts frail
for the task at hand, the ritual digging.
I need an ancient shovel, big handled.
One stored indoors through winter. One
from old iron and solid oak. Tru-tested.
Someone else's that rests, no longer
needed, hid in some basement corner
it's keeper exhausted from digging.
I find this, my shovel, at a garage sale
leaning, pinned behind a dented Schwinn
blade down, standing on its rusty head.

II.

So, with shovel slung across my shoulder, I start
off for a piece of level ground, buoyed by a passion
for resolution and cock-sure I'll know it when
I see it. Quick-stepping down the soft-trodden path
past woody knolls, small clearings, split-rail fences
down by the retention pond, still and quiet, then
toward the woods— a flat and serene place. I'll take it.
I thrust my shovel in, hit stone. It's echoes reverberate
back up the path like rabbits hopping, multiplying.
The brook, like a possum's tail, trails from the pond
into the woods, wagging its cadence, whispering

III.

the easy truths— smooth, clear and shallow:
You can have it all . . . Reality is 90% appearance . . .
There are two kinds of people . . . Better him than me . . .
One-time won't hurt anything . . . Dark, damp, rocky—
I deserve better than this. My bones warrant more
than this low ground, shady and rank. My eternity
my eternal peace, jostled by roaring water and worms.
Here, this dank ground; this plot, this loose, gritty soil
unfit for digging anything durable. Unfit for holes.

IV.
VMMG@www.mom.com
Dear Mom,

      Have been thinking much of you lately. Don't know
why. I am working my garden. Stopped for some lunch (tomato
soup and grilled cheese— just like you used to make). You come
to me as I gaze out the window at the pond. A heron is catching
frogs near the bank. He stands so still on his legs of straw.
I know it is the seasons that bring him back, repeating familiar
lessons. I see the heron in me now, the seasons in your smiles.

V.
I didn't see the sense in a fence anymore
nor did gampa Alan, my neighbor.
We planned our work, worked our plan—
his block, steel pipe, length of chain;
my trusty shovel, wheel barrow, tin snips
wrench, screw drivers, and pipe cutter.
First, we freed the chain-link fencing.
Ivy vines, tree roots, silver maple saplings
entwined, embedded, ensnarled, held
the fence, pulled and twisted and tore at
the fence. We eased and cajoled, snipped
and tugged, together freed the linked fence.
We cut the horizontal head pipe running
across the post tops, planted the lengths
like flag poles or giant antenna in the lawn.
Last, we took the posts. Cutting's not good
enough for posts; they must be ripped-out.
Al cleared the dirt and roots from each post
footing and double wrapped the post-chain
preventing slippage. I positioned the block
snug against the post, angled the steel pipe

through the loop of chain and leveraged
all afternoon, leaving a trail of post holes
expiated regrets and fears. Then it rained.

VI.
And, sweat pours across my face
as if spirit were a muscle, releasing
the juice of agony after hard labor,
or an eye that weeps from long trial.
A warm breeze blows gently, down
upon my wet face. And, the sky
becomes that familiar portrait
I would come to know, want to know.
My face dries in that soft wind
Veronica, Veronica, Veronica . . .

VII.
It could've been the rain,
tears or sweat, but it's
Mia culpa, mia maxima culpa—
the deep red of blood
beading in the sun.
The double helix of desire,
Deus Ex Machina—
both flesh and spirit
forever at each other's throat
turning. Here is the falling
down where one would rise
and sing, and be glad . . .
Instead, stumbling
beneath this breath's weight
which reddens my blood.

VIII.
O, how they howl and wail
bodies rock and flail
noisy is the empty pail.
Grief's clothes borrowed
sorrowful sorrow
What about tomorrow?
What about tomorrow?

IX.
When I climb back up the hill for lunch
my knees ache, a mist shadows my house.
The old shovel becomes a crutch.
I can't shoulder its heavy head,
can't cradle its unbalanced height,
I lean on it as it leaned on me.
We work our way along the path
together at last; neither can go it
alone. I try sending the shovel
ahead, but it waits like an old dog.
Uncertain and uneasy by separation
it brings me back again to my knees.

X.
More than beast and less than kind.
Here I face myself in the mirror
set naked and alone. I can't stare
directly anymore. Even my feet
seem strange among smooth hairs
ears, eye jellies, tongue and bone.
My skin soft as a worn leather coat
hangs looser than memory, drawn
by the ravages of linear time
from forehead to gut to my hips
translucent lines stream
in a universe of sons and cycles.

XI.
The summer after second grade
I slipped running and trapped my foot
anchored beneath a chain link fence.
My brother, Chris, was right there.
He bent the fence and freed my foot.
You can call him, I'll give you his #.
I took four stitches in Petoskey.
My screams still crash like waves.
I can't even imagine being crucified.

XII.
The foundation, walls and entry secure
no more need be done. Perhaps,
I can sleep now. Really sleep. Sleep
the sleep of resolution.
                         Not an infant's
sleep, waking and re-waking every hour
quick for the bottle and song.
                         No.
A sleep that descends with certainty
across my past. One that opens onto
a moonlit lawn, pines and the pond
illuminated by
              the chaos of night.
I have need to dig but one grave like this.
Yet, this employment, this continual
digging and scraping and moving about
of dirt likes me well
                      gives me rest.
Now I must embrace the inevitable.
Now I will till my future garden.

XIII.
By the time she enters the second grade
the sunflowers of September will tower
in pursuit of chasing that descending sun.
Their cheeks full of seeds nearly burst
with seasoned knowledge. Meghan
will be seven, I'll own more gray hairs,
and we'll make a picture that first morning
standing in front of those brave, obedient—
Yes— sunflowers that dare to chase the sun.

XIV.
This October I will harvest flowers
like my parents in their Octobers.
I will till the beds one last time.
My basement full of drying flowers
strung by their heels in bunches
they hang from joist hooks. By March
their seeds will be as ready as ever—
then I will seek-out my reliable shovel.

"Big Dreams," colored pencil, Linda K. Sienkiewicz, 1996.

Linda K. Sienkiewicz
What Matters

What Matters

The ferris wheel takes me up and
drops me in a soaring nose-dive.
Trapped, I've gone 'round enough
not to wail at this mad amusement
or throw my heart like a red flare.

If the season doesn't change,
if the toaster doesn't burn my bagel,
if the fortune teller's arm doesn't fall off
before my card comes up,
I will know what matters.

The night burns in a calliope of colors.
Wrapped in blue flannel, I wait for safe landing.
All I really want is you.

Linda K. Sienkiewicz

Anaconda

He tastes the air,
tongue flicking,
and catches my scent.
He slides across
my belly and
around my breasts.
Like a steel rope,
he wraps each leg
and slowly parts them.
I am captive,
the one charmed,
my back pressed
against jaguar skins.
Hypnotized,
I cannot move
or make a sound.
Fangs unsheathed,
ready to strike,
he is a muscle,
iridescent black
and gold design.
His grip tightens,
the sky purples.
The jungle is
a white strobe in
shuddering sheets,
an Amazon storm.
I take a breath—
in one swift lunge,
he swallows
my wild pulse.

Linda K. Sienkiewicz

Toronto Trolley

Out the window, a smorgasbord blurs past,
Rooneem's Bakery, Wong's Fruit Market,
Alagonquin Sweet Grass Factory.
In the aisle, a loud jangle. Silver chains
and black leather muscle alongside me

followed by an orange-haired girl, thin
as a cigarette, rings in her nose, lips and brow.
We make room, grab the same silver pole.
A Vietnamese man slips into the seat
next to the Malaysian woman in red.

They search for common native words
but fall into broken English. The man struggles
to tell of his years in a U.S. refugee camp,
having to show his need for political asylum.

So you can stay, you know? You got to have proof.
Five years it took, he repeats. *You got to prove.*
His point made, he says *Bye* just like that, jumps
out at Spadina and runs to the Prague Deli.
The trolley lurches, we sway in unison.

Linda K. Sienkiewicz

Nightly Grind

A demolition crew from hell
brandishing thunderous jackhammers
crashes the bedroom ceiling
with earsplitting destruction and blasts
my idyllic dream of a *Bride Magazine* marriage.

Grinding and gnashing drill holes in my sleep
far deeper than my father's snore,
a nasal cacophony of deep sea rumbles
that stretched thin my mother's endurance.

I wake in horror to my new groom
whose obnoxious molar-crushing habit
threatens to pulverize his teeth to grit.
It quakes my flesh to the very DNA
and the honeymoon's not even over.

His noise rocks the bed, chisels panic
in my heart. I scream for him to stop,
scream he's ruining everything. He
barely opens his eyes, mumbles something
about a bad bite and turns over.

Six thousand nights pass; I still dream
of jackhammers or the screech of six-feet-tall,
thick-necked woodpeckers drilling metal trees.
Sometimes I lie awake, wonder if
I could fix that bad bite
with a swift kick in the teeth.

Linda K. Sienkiewicz

Order Toll-Free

I can draw like a professional, instantly
with the Easy Reflection Sketcher
and have fun expressing myself
with rainbowed self-stick labels.
I will no longer lose sleep
over shifting slipping mattresses;
I can rest as I pedal pounds away
and firm those facial muscles
while I sleep or watch t.v.
I'll be like new and I can charge it,
easily, quickly, gently.

Shopping with Walter Drake,
I can enjoy incredible savings
on gadgets
that add years to my shaver's life,
train a wayward toe,
vacuum blackheads,
eject cookies,
split pills,
zap pests,
kill odors,
improve, protect, enhance, relieve,
all in half the time,
and personalized.

I want to look smart and worry-free
in every decorator color,
one size to fit me.
Walter, I want my life
money-back guaranteed.

Cosmic Misconnection

We meditate over incense fires,
inhale a divine bouquet of inspirations
from the East, squint at rainbow
auras while humming mantras.

Ron babbles about a far-out dimension
where man's future is cosmically scribed.
Viv says she is going to find it
through transcendental travel.
The Mahareshi trips the switch
to illuminate our minds
and Baba Ram Dass' sacred cookbook
has us become one with a candleflame.
After the Year of the Earth Monkey,
everyone says their lives changed.

I meditate till I hyperventilate
and lose my way in the astral plane;
I never embrace the universe as one
and can't transcend my ego. I wonder
if a yellow smiley face is pasted
like a third eye on my forehead.
Even earnest prayer at the Evangelical
United Brethren Church fails to transport me.
I don't get it.

So, I pack all that searching desire
for cosmic consciousness in a box
with my Carlos Castanada book collection.
Not to worry. Ram Dass says
The most exquisite paradox is—
when you give it up, you can have it all.
I give it up.

Linda K. Sienkiewicz

Smile, Baby

Snapshot smiles beam
of first love.
A long-haired boy
in embroidered jeans hugs
a polkadot mini-clad me;
rose-tinted granny glasses
perch on my shining face
that turns to his
like a flower to the sun.

I see the playful ecstacy,
now long faded, that rocked
me seasick, his wild
antics and loopy screaming love
dizzy as the car and me
spinning donuts crazy
in the snow.

Our insides flipped
in his dad's old Rambler
slammed into fifth gear
airborne over the dip
in Hillside Road and
from each kiss
deep enough
to swallow whole
like I did the dream
of a baby, ours.
We were drunk
with love love love
and Ripple. Such
wide-eyed smiles,
a shutter-blink ago.

Linda K. Sienkiewicz

Jackie Junior

Jackie Jr., my best friend, was a boy
but I didn't care. Red-haired and freckly,
he'd stand outside my door hollerin' for me.
I'd bounce out and we headed for the woods.

Jackie taught me how to fly. I hugged that hangin' vine
like he showed, and he sent me swingin' across
the ravine so fast I thought my head'd pop off.
Then we swang till our hands got blisters.

Sometimes we played army by the stinky creek.
Jackie always said he was from Ireland, and me,
I was the blonde spy from Sweden. We'd fight
the invisible Commies and beat 'em every time.

Jackie never treated me different 'cause I was a girl,
but once he dared me to tightrope-walk across the gorge
on a slippy-smooth tree bridge. No chicken girl,
I said *double dare.* When we got halfway over

it was the best. We stayed all day sittin' in the sky,
legs hangin'. He was Tarzan (with a lisp), and me,
I was Cheetah (This was better than Jane, Jackie said.
Jane couldn't climb trees or swing on vines).

Then there was this one stuffy summer night.
We were kinda older, and firefly catchin' somehow
got us in a slap fight. We chased each other 'round
like mad, tearin' up the front lawns, laughin'

smack, smack and *smack you back.* Jackie
pushed me down, all outta breath and hottish
and wrestled me in the sweaty grass. He squeezed
my arms and did a kiss on my face.

I ran home, my t-shirt torn, arms sting-y red,
and Mother said I shouldn't play that way no more.
Wasn't nice, she said, and her eyebrows pinched together.
I didn't know what the heck she meant.

Besides, I kinda liked this queer new feeling
and how my heart got all pumpy. And all that night
I tore around with Jackie Jr. in my dreams,
him just catchin' me again and again and again.

Linda K. Sienkiewicz

Girlfriend

For Nancy

We talk in a nonstop, four day rush
like girls squeezed in a bathroom stall
who share a smoke before the last bell.
Over Amaretto coffee and popovers
in your St. Paul apartment this time,
we belly laugh over our kids and
howl dirty jokes about ex-husbands.

You frosted my hair in the tenth grade,
loaned me your lavender hot pants and
listened to me sob over true love's madness.
You took my bitching when I felt unloved.
You are as dear to me as my left pinky,
real as a bowl of minestrone.

We comb your high school diaries.
I wonder if I was written in them
as often as you were in mine.
Did you miss me like I missed you
when you were sent to boarding school?
Did you hate me when I broke the heel
on your velvet platform shoes?

Then from your diary pages you unfold,
carefully as a pressed paper heartbeat,
an ancient sketch I made of your foot.

Linda K. Sienkiewicz

Sleepwalker

Second to the right and then
straight on till morning,
my son wanders alone
in another place, a different time,
turning the invisible pages
of a happily-ever-after fairy tale.
I sleep in my tennis shoes,
one ear tuned for the nonsensical jabber
that precedes his vacant-eyed walk
down the hallway to the stairs.

I wonder if he's searching for
some once-upon-a-time land
where fairy mothers give three wishes,
not a scolding when the day gets long.
I fear he might decide to stay
lost in the Land of Giants, or follow
the town musicians to Bremen
and never want to come back.

Each night I give him my kiss
to wear on a chain around his neck.
I wish I had a magic mirror
to let me step into his dreams
or a wooden shoe to rock him in,
sailing on the misty sea.
Up all night, I am
on the other side of his journey.

Tied

Linda K. Sienkiewicz

Like a monster 4x4 snowplow,
you scrape my puny body
along the asphalt into a ditch
with a mere punch in a pillow,
that particular look you get,
or with the shoes you
hard-ball pitch into the closet
where I cower, starved
without the right words,
finding only crumbs
in the pockets of hung pants.

I hang from your
heavy-starched shirt-sleeves
like a puppet
in this small dark space.
I imagine you a beast,
myself brave enough
to shoot only little pea balls
at your hoary back.

I believe you to be a freight train.
Black coffee smoke puffs
from your cheeks.
I tie my sanity
to the tracks
and scream.

Linda K. Sienkiewicz

Running With That Dream

I dream of wild-eyed women,
run through pre-dawn streets with them,
my eyes luminescent as angel fish
that sleep in a lake of shining mercury.
They call me to drink from it
with mother's porcelain tea cup,
fly out the door of the car that won't start,
jump off the neverending staircase,
run past the man who shouts as if I cannot hear
and soar above torn alleys that lead nowhere.

I listen to the cries of ten caged songbirds
that peck and peck but never break through
the ice of frozen foods in the supermarket.
Peas and carrots in identical, white paper boxes
wait to be released from such exact rows.
With a Swiss army knife, I slit the packages,
spill the insides, set them rolling free in the aisles
and dance on them in my bare feet.

I dance and run all night long
through endless dreams of unsung songs
with a thousand raging sisters.

Linda K. Sienkiewicz

Coming Off Zoloft

Alone at the corner table in the Coffee Exchange,
I write furiously, pause only to gulp
hazelnut decaf or stab an apple tart loaded with
macadamias, almonds, cashews and caramel.
Each day further from my last dose of Zoloft,
I scribble increasingly more.

Today, apples and nuts sink like lead
because my eyes take in more
than I can stomach, anti-anti-depressanted.

My family says they can't talk to me anymore,
won't reach out to a pacing mother
whose bite slices their tender flesh.

Here, people smile cordially, secure
in their roles, to serve or sip coffee.
Glass jars sit in smug rows—each
coffee bean, a little eye to watch me.

I want to throw macadamia nuts
at the man so intent on reading his paper,
scream at the couple holding hands
while they drink cappuccino through paper straws.
My hazelnut turns cold and bitter
but I'm afraid to go home where
my thoughts run in place like
that man's feet keeping time to music;
I wish I were a radio. I'd switch stations.

Six cakes in the display case tempt me.
One flaunts ripe cherries glistening
on sexy whipped cream mountains.

Linda K. Sienkiewicz

Sex was a drag taking Zoloft.
I tried Pamelor; it made my mouth
taste like an oily lugnut—
like kissing my own transmission.
Prozac, so smooth,
ironed my sex life flat as a table.
I thought Zoloft would be better.
Two months later, I'm too blue.

I'm drowning in this coffeepot
and there's no exit sign.
If I could go home now, maybe
my kids would say they missed me.
I'd bake apple pie and nutmeat tarts.
I'd sweep apple peels off the counter
and make love
to George right there
on the speckled formica.

All-Night Movie

Linda K. Sienkiewicz

She slips from her plaid pajamas and vanishes
to a dream where her first love returns.
He looks just like the first time she saw him,
a seventeen-year-old cowboy
striding through the high school doors
into her heart. They dance again
under crepe paper streamers in the gym.

She doesn't want to come down from this dream
to yesterday's crusted dishes,
the dog scratching to go out
and in and out again, or the husband
who is just there, always there.

She remembers her dream boy so well,
the one with kisses of melting butter,
his smooth face oversplashed with Brut.
She has taken to naps on the sofa
to hurry the long hours till night.

Awake, she imagines his face on the tall boy
packing bags at Sparkle Market,
on the dark-haired repairman
who doesn't have the right parts
to fix the dishwasher. He stars
in the All-Night Movie, another musical
with Fred twirling Ginger.

In bed, she rests her spinning head
on her husband's chest and settles in
to his heartbeat. She remembers
the first time she slept with him,
the strength she once drew
from his earthly presence.

She drifts into a dream of him
where he waits inside an open door.
He offers familiar whiskered kisses,
early morning passion on rumpled sheets,
toast and a tango in the kitchen.

His breath in her ear,
his roots already in her dream,
he isn't Fred or
the boy at Sparkle Market,
but he makes her heart twirl.

Linda K. Sienkiewicz

Tattooed in Jocko's Parlor

(King's Cross, U.K.)

No, darlin', it don't hurt a bit, he spits
in his London accent. He grins
like a bearded weasel, too fat
to get off his stool. He stubs out his cig
and sticks out his tongue,
behold—the Cross of Jesus.

I step back, split between my desire
and the fear of swarming needles.
Jocko whistles to the woman
dressed in beads and lace
flipping through his book of designs.
Show her your titty, Lila.
I wince at the flower petals
tattooed around her nipple.
I need a mug of Guiness.

I look at Jocko's inked skin
stretched over flabby arms,
shoulders, neck, earlobes
and who knows where else.
I think of the hook pain has;
the adrenaline buzz that sends you
hovering six inches from the ceiling.
Detached from your chosen torture
you become worthy of something
beautiful no one can take away.

I throw up in his sink
and jet home to the States,
smug with my souvenir.
Now I'm wondering
if my daisy needs a bee.

Linda K. Sienkiewicz

Danger in Perfect Order

Bent over to inspect Grade A Medium Eggs
for cracks, I am assaulted
by English Muffins. They jump off
the shelf and onto the back of my head.
The hit is just a soft suprise.
I carefully place them in my cart
next to the eggs and Lumberjack bread.
I have everything in place.

But English Muffins, or other baked goods,
don't often fall on my head in Pick 'n' Pay
just as men don't often write me poetry.
Yet these things happen, momentarily
upsetting order. And I wonder
about the exact placement of life's
circumstances, why I am here,
not there, why I pick six cans of tomato sauce,
why I ignore the fat-free chips on sale
or marry a man who buys me Hallmark cards.

What is returnable once opened?
Every choice, every step is fraught with danger.
Even on the way home, a soft loaf of bread
could flatten under a bag of rolling apples
with damage beyond repair.

Linda K. Sienkiewicz

Kiss the Sun

I'm shakin' my world
    like a bumble bee in a jar.
Got it tied to a paddle
    with a rubber band.
Whap, whap, whap!

I spin like a wild dervish,
    subsist on sky peaches,
bathe in the Nile,
    kiss the sun.

I'm a jumping jack
    on the kitchen table.
The salt and pepper dance
    right outta their shakers.

I grab the ears
    and bite the nose
    of the invisible man under the bed.
I'm growing wings
    where my arms were cut off
    and I'm flying;
I'm gone, really gone.

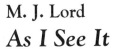

M. J. Lord
As I See It

When You Picture Me, What Do You See?

I don't form a picture, or an image in my mind.
You have a myriad of qualities that I seek,
and usually find.
I know you by your voice,
if we've talked for awhile.
I can tell if you're down, or tired.
Sometimes, I can hear you smile.
I know you by your gestures,
or the touch of your hand.
By the height of your voice,
I know how tall you stand.
I'd know you almost anywhere,
though in a crowd, you're hard to recognize.
You are perceived as who you are,
when seen through my eyes.

M. J. Lord

My Fingers Do the Walking

Let your fingers do the walking,
the Yellow Pages ad invites.
My fingers do a lot more than walk.
They read, write,
scrub, travel, caress, examine,
and experience a lifetime
of sensations.

They read novels, poems,
magazine articles and more.

My fingers write stories
as they instinctively press keys
to form words and paragraphs.

They have scrubbed and polished
floors, counter tops and furniture,
finding unseen sticky spots, and
implements of daily life left
out of place.

They travel over mountain ranges,
rivers, lakes and seas
as they
investigate
tactile maps of
the United States, South America, and beyond.

They caress hands, identify
those of my husband, relatives
and friends. My fingers recognize
them by texture of skin, presence

or absence of ring, hair, callous,
length of fingernail, and size.
They caress the silky hair of
pets, and the soft skin of infants.

They examine linen dresses, art,
roses, Bonsai trees, electric sockets,
surfaces, and other objects. Identify
tacos by weight, temperature, size,
texture, and consistency.

My fingers have experienced
a lifetime of intimacy and
exploration, almost touching
the untouchable.

M. J. Lord

Front Hooker

Like an endless parade
of colorful pairs of Siamese twins,
they hang etched in lace on plastic hangers.
Small paper tags smugly announce my size.

I examine one after another:
those that hook in front,
those with one, two
and three hooks in back,
underwire, sports design, strapless,
with and without bows,
black, red, purple, blue,
green, beige, white,
silk, lace, cotton, nylon,
Fruit Of The Loom, *MaidenForm*,
Hanes, *Playtex*,
Cross Your Heart.
And of course, the *Wonder Bra*,
carefully designed to enhance
woman's natural form.
Should I wonder if a
simple bra will be enough,
I can try the Miracle Bra.
Are there really miracles?

I examine the possibilities,
knowing I should choose
a white cotton underwire.
I choose a red lace front hooker
and wonder if it will transform me.

M. J. Lord

Silence

Silence fills my sleeping house,
embraces me with its calming presence.
Then my alarm clock rudely breaks in,
disturbs the peace with its discord.
I sit up slowly and hit the snooze.
My mind races.
What day is it?
What was I dreaming?
What's on my schedule?
And the silence says nothing.
I turn on the news.
A woman was raped.
As I push the off button,
the silence echoes the reporter's words.
Alone, I ponder life's options,
and the silence speaks what I'm afraid to think.
Later that day, I go to a concert;
the music is loud.
When I leave, hours later,
the silence deafens me.
I lay awake late into the night.
Voices from the day scream in my head,
and piercing silence calls out to me.

Summer Round Up

The sign on the door said, "Mary-Jo Kaiser and Colleen McNitte."

"Same sign as last year," my mother said.

"Same door," my father added.

"The other girl hasn't arrived yet," Mrs. Knight said, not acknowledging my parents' comments, or the fact that she knew Colleen and me from last year.

My heart sank instantly. All of the excitement and anxious anticipation that I had been feeling for the past few days disappeared. With Mrs. Knight's few cold words, all of the unpleasant memories of Summer Round Up filled my mind.

It was the summer of 1974, and I was eleven years old. This would be my second year to participate in the School for the Blind's Summer Round Up program. For the next five weeks, Colleen and I, (and other blind and partially-sighted kids) would be instructed in Mobility, Art, Physical Education, and Activities of Daily Living. We would live in dormitory-style cottages, and go home for weekends.

"Dinner will be in the main dining hall tonight but, after that, you kids will eat here in the cottage," Mrs. Knight was saying. "Dinner on Sundays will be cold sandwiches, since parents can bring kids back until seven o'clock. We don't want to prepare a hot meal for too many kids. I have the money that you sent in an envelope, and you will be given a quarter each day, so that you can go to social hour from four to five. You can buy candy and pop there. We'll have to take whatever you haven't eaten before dinner time, and we will keep it in the kitchen. When you want it, you will have to ask us for it. If you brought any snacks with you, I will need to lock them up as well."

I held my breath, hoping that my parents would remember not to say anything about the candy and chips that Mom packed for me.

They didn't, and Mrs. Knight talked on and on about bedtime, chores, and bathing.

Finally, she left, and Mom began unpacking my things. She hid the snacks in a drawer under my rain hat, cards, and radio. I knew that my mother could never find a place to hide them that was safe from the intrusive eyes and prying fingers of Mrs. Knight and the other staff. I remembered in horror how Rose, one of the counselors, had found a box of candy in my room last year. She had taken it, and I wasn't allowed to go to social hour for the rest of the week. They kept the candy until my parents brought me back the next Sunday.

As my mother put my clothes away, she talked on and on about remembering to set my hair, brush my teeth and ask if my clothes were dirty at the end of the day. I began to feel funny. A part of me wanted Colleen and my other friends to arrive and our parents to leave. On the other hand, I was beginning to feel homesick. Mrs. Knight wasn't the only nasty staff person. That place was full of them. To make matters worse, Cheryl and some of the other weirdos would probably be back. Cheryl still wet her pants and always smelled. She wore braces on her legs and walked slowly. The counselors used to make us take turns walking to classes with her. Cheryl wasn't the only one in the group that smelled. There was Terry, who wet the bed at least once a week and took three days to change the sheets. One time, they made Colleen and me help her change the bed. I remembered how Mrs. Yale, the Activities Of Daily Living teacher, tried to stop me from taking all of my clothes home every weekend. I nearly burst into tears as I remembered the time that Mrs. Knight accused Colleen and me of playing "dirty doctor." We had taken a chair with wheels on it from the play room. We were in our room playing "hospital." We were taking turns being the nurse and patient, wheeling each other around the room, and getting in and out of bed. Mrs. Knight had threatened to tell the principal of the school and, worse yet, our parents. She said that what we were doing was an embarrassment to the school.

As my mother put the last of my clothes away, Colleen and some of the other girls started to arrive. Our parents talked while Colleen's mother unpacked her things. Colleen and I caught up on the past year and giggled and whispered about all of the secrets that we had to share. Thankfully, Mary Anne and Sarah had also returned and were rooming across the hall. Some of our other friends had also returned, and some of the new kids seemed okay. Of course, Cheryl, Terry, and some of the other weirdos had returned, along with some new ones. When Colleen's things were put away, we hugged and kissed our parents good-bye.

I shut the door to our room as one of the new weirdos walked past our room shrieking, "aaay, aaay." As I climbed from a chair to the desk to hide my snacks and extra money in the "secret place," Colleen began spraying the room with deodorant. "This place stinks!" she exclaimed shaking the aerosol can.

The snacks secured in the cupboard above my closet, I got out a bottle of perfume, and sprayed my side of the room. As the new weirdo passed our room again chanting, "aaay, aaay," Colleen and I began adjusting to institutional living.

Our first class in the morning was Mobility/Library. Each instructor was assigned two students per group. We would have forty-five minutes of Mobility each. My instructor was Dawn, and I had Mobility first. We worked on Street Crossing, and Orientation to New Buildings. I was reluctant to use my cane properly. It was a folding cane that I had been given the previous fall when I'd begun attending my neighborhood school. That summer, Virginia, one of the counselors, had shown me her folding cane, and I had wanted one more than anything else. Now I had one of my own. In fact, I was the only kid in the program to have a folding cane, and there was no way that I was going to ruin my tip on those sidewalks. Dawn had quickly given me a straight cane to use for the summer.

While Dawn worked with Sam, a boy from our group, I went to the library. I loved that time, because all of the books were in a format that I could listen to or read. We also went on some field trips. We toured the capital building and the nature center.

At the capital building, we actually stood outside of the governor's office and sat in the chairs in the room where the State Senators and Representatives met. We had a lot of fun feeling the old doors, carved columns, and the glass and marble floors. We all banged on the replica of the Liberty Bell, and Sam licked it. At the nature center, we looked at different trees and leaves. We saw the museum with stuffed wild animals.

Our second and favorite class of the day was Art. Of course, the boys went to shop, but we were sure that we had more fun. Mr. Tom always gave us lemonade at the beginning of class, and we started and ended each class with singing. Sometimes, we would sing while working on our projects.

After lunch each day, Colleen and I would go outside and sit on the glider and sing the songs that we had learned. Sometimes, Sarah and Mary Anne would join us. The glider squeaked loudly, so we would sing at the top of our lungs to try and drown it out. We were right under the window to the cottage for the blind deaf kids, and their house mother would repeatedly reprimand us for being too loud. One time she announced angrily, "My kids need to take a nap, and they can't sleep with all your racket!"

"If they are deaf," I asked innocently, "then how can they hear us?" Colleen giggled, and the house mother sighed in exasperation and went back to her cottage. That evening, Mrs. Knight told us that the glider next door was off-limits to our program.

In the afternoons, we had Gym and Activities Of Daily Living. In Gym, competition was fierce among some of us. We competed against each other and tried to beat our own records in track, gymnastics and swimming. We were all the best at something, and we wanted to be the best at everything.

In Activities Of Daily Living, we learned some basic cooking, sewing and personal grooming skills. And how could I forget, we learned how to make those dreaded hospital corners. Every Friday, we would change our beds and dust and mop before going home. Mrs. Yale would inspect our beds and rooms, and everything had to be perfect or she would threaten to keep us from going home until we got it right. Colleen and I quickly mastered hospital corners our first year. Mrs. Yale still argued with me about what clothing I should take home with me on weekends. I didn't see her point. I wasn't asking her to carry my things to the bus.

Every afternoon, we went to social hour, or to a grocery store near campus. Colleen, who still had a lot of usable vision, quickly secured an off-campus pass from her Mobility instructor. In fact, she was the only girl in our cottage to get one during the entire five weeks. Off-campus passes were usually a privilege given to the older kids. She could take one person with her, so we went almost every day. With Colleen's pass and my extra money, we had quite the smorgasbord hidden behind the magazines in the secret cupboard.

A few times a week, either before or after dinner, five or six of us would have to take Patty, the chanting weirdo, to the health center to get her Ritalin. The counselors hated taking her, so they would put it off until we would practically have to pull her off the ceiling to get her there. Colleen and another partially-sighted girl would have to try and direct us, and the rest of us would have to try to keep Patty walking and on the sidewalk. She would usually scream and cry the whole way there. At other times, she would chant "aaay, aaay!" We were stopped more than once by staff from other programs to see what we were doing to "that poor girl." I'm sure we were a comical sight, but we found the whole thing annoying.

Every evening after dinner, we had recreation. We swam, roller skated, bowled and played games. Each week, we had a special activity. We had scavenger hunts, relays and a mini-fair.

Bedtime was at nine. Mrs. Anderson, the night house mother, was pretty cool. She would usually let us talk until ten if we didn't keep anyone awake. On a few hot nights, she'd let us sit in the hall for awhile to try and cool off. Inevitably, we would all end up in one room talking, which defeated the whole purpose. Mrs. Anderson would pretend not to notice for up to half an hour, and then she would send us back to our own rooms.

Although they did a pretty good job of segregating the boys from the girls, we still had some activities together and our paths crossed during free time. A boy named Marvin had the worst crush on me. I didn't really like him much. Although he seemed smart enough, he was just weird. Colleen said that he looked weird and he talked funny. Of course, he told everyone that I was his girlfriend. I didn't want to hurt his feelings so, when he asked me to the pizza party at his cottage on the last night of the program, I accepted. The last year Tim, a boy that I really liked, had asked me, and Mrs. Knight had refused to let me go. I figured that accepting Marvin's invitation was safe, since she would probably do the same this year. Much to my chagrin, Mrs. Knight announced at dinner the night before the party that this year our entire cottage had been invited to participate in the boy's pizza party and that we would all be allowed to attend.

On the last night of Summer Round Up, we had a talent show. While all of the other kids were singing "Billy Don't Be a Hero" and "Michael Rowed the Boat Ashore", Colleen and I did "The Streak At TSB." We made up our own words and had been practicing for weeks. Our act was the talk of the program before we ever hit the stage.

After the show, we went to the pizza party, and then we had an all-night party in our cottage.

The next day, we were all exhausted and ready to go home. We went to our classes for one last time, said good-bye to all of our friends and went home with our parents.

When I think about the two summers that I spent at TSB, I realize that I learned a lot more than cane travel, daily living skills, and how to make slippers. I experienced the feeling of autonomy in choosing what to wear, how to do my hair and what recreational activities to enjoy. Through living and talking with other kids, I learned how different people's expectations could be, depending on where one lived and went to school. I felt safe in the knowledge that I knew how to swim and would be unlikely to drown in deep water. I experienced the freedom of running as fast as I could, unassisted. And, right or wrong, I was given several unspoken messages. As I saw things, it was okay to break rules as long as I didn't get caught. I experienced the benefits and consequences of challenging authority. Based on the actions of our counselors, I learned that if I put something off long enough someone else will do it. The message came through loud and clear that expectations are different for boys and girls. I discovered it isn't always what I do that counts, it's how it is perceived. And, finally, I learned to expect the unexpected.

Our Ferdy

I named him Ferdinand, because I liked the name. I heard a baby-sitter talking about a Ferdinand somebody or other once, when she was studying history.

I was ten when we brought him home from an old farmhouse. The sign in front had said, *FREE KITTENS*. We begged our parents to stop and promised to take care of a new kitty. We would feed it and clean its poop box and everything, if they would just "Please, please, please, let us have a kitten!" Reluctantly, our parents agreed to just stop and look. Half an hour later, we were on our way home with Ferdy.

Ferdy was completely black. Even the roof of his mouth was black. In the dark, he was scary! All we could see were his glowing, yellow eyes and glistening white teeth.

Ferdy wasn't much of a pet, but he was our Ferdy, and we loved him. He ran whenever the doorbell or phone rang. He never wanted to be held, and he was always slipping outside. Ferdy had a certain knack for getting into fights and coming home all banged up. A few times, he came home with big infected sores that covered the entire side of his face and head. I still remember the strong unmistakable odor those sores gave off when Mom lanced them. It was enough to make me gag, but he was our Ferdy.

One day, we came home from school and found our mother furiously poking tiny threads of the living room sheers back in place with a needle. She said Ferdinand had ruined her sheers, and he had to go.

We cried on the way to the Humane Society. Ferdy howled and urinated the whole way there. We were told to wait in the car, and they took Ferdy, our Ferdy, inside. I wanted to run after them and scream, "Don't let them kill our Ferdy!" but I knew that I couldn't. When they came back to the car, Mom told us Ferdy had a new home. She said the vet gave him a shot to help him relax. She told us that if nobody took our Ferdy in the next few days they would keep him as their special pet. I remember believing her, wanting to believe her. Through a flood of tears and disillusionment, I truly believed that our Ferdy, with his pus-filled face and urine smell, was going to become a special pet of the Human Society.

Deposit And Retrieve

I awake to a trail of deposits from my fourteen-year-old retriever. As I am forced into semi-consciousness, I pull the covers over my head, hope they will shield me from reality.

Eventually, the pungent aroma penetrates my cotton and wool fortress. Reluctantly, I pull the covers back and sit up. Toes curl inward toward the balls of my feet, as they are shocked to life by cold air. I place them on the cool carpet uncertainly, unsure how close the offensive objects might be to my bed.

I move hesitantly forward, as Mandy slowly gets up, shakes, and prances unsteadily toward the door. I continue to inch my way forward, investigative toes carefully checking carpet for safe places to set feet.

I let her outside, grab paper towel and bag, and prepare for my early morning scavenger hunt. As I examine each inch of floor space, picking up treasures along the way, the putrid odor assaults my nostrils, forces my mind to imagine my house is being taken over by far more deposits than my dog would ever be capable of producing.

When at last I am satisfied I haven't missed any stragglers, I open the door to let her back in. I call her name shrilly into the cold dark windy morning, "MANDY," and hope that her nearly deaf ears might hear. I flicker the lights in an attempt to catch the attention of her cataract-glazed eyes.

Finally, I put my coat on over my night gown, slip my feet into last night's high heels, and step outside to retrieve her.

Reading Out Loud

As a child, nothing could compare to the fear and anxiety I experienced at even the possibility of being called on to read in front of the class. Admittedly, I spent a lot of time sitting in corners, in the hall, and being asked to stay inside during recess. Although these punishments were unpleasant, they were not devastating enough to end the behaviors which put me in unsatisfactory positions. If every time I talked back, chewed gum in class, took things that weren't mine and swore, I was asked to read a passage from my reader to the class, these behaviors might have been curbed entirely.

In school, my teachers seemed oblivious to the terror they could invoke in me by saying, "Mary-Jo, will you read the next page?"

I fantasized about being able to read with the intonation, clarity, and speed my teachers and classmates demonstrated. I read and re-read passages from my textbooks, hoping to get it right.

I'd just about have a passage memorized, and then it would happen. I'd be asked to read a passage from another text. I'd break out in a cold sweat, and the room would spin in all directions. I'd be sure the entire school was listening as I'd begin to read haltingly. I'd stumble over, mispronounce, and skip words. Each phrase would come out strained and sound more like a question than a statement, as I forced my mouth and tongue to shape each word. At the end of each assigned passage, I would feel humiliated and grateful the ordeal was over.

So when I said "I'm going to a coffee house where I won't know anyone and I don't even drink coffee" and then added "to read my poetry out loud," it shocked everybody. So why was I going to a coffee house to read in front of strangers?

Today as a writer, I enjoy the works of others, particularly when they are read by the writers. Although I enjoy hearing good readers read my work, I often feel frustrated when they don't read a piece as I imagine it. I've come to the realization that the only person who can read my work exactly as I like it is me. I need to start somewhere.

Going to coffee houses gives me opportunities to hear poetry and prose read by writers. It also helps me practice reading my work.

I have been reading in public for over two years. Now, when I walk into a coffee house, I know most of the people there. Although I still don't like coffee, after a couple of shots of espresso, I can read anything. I still stumble over and miss words, or read phrases incorrectly. I'm working on developing a comfortable reading speed, but I no longer feel self-conscious about reading. At times, that childhood fear creeps up, but it is overshadowed by the satisfaction and pride I feel when I'm able to share my work with you.

M. J. Lord

Wrapped in Rhetoric

Let's look at some of the terms used to described the disabled population: *persons with disabilities, handicapped, handicappers, physically challenged, physically handicapped, physically impaired, disabled, hearing impaired, hard of hearing, profoundly deaf, deaf, legally blind, visually impaired, sight impaired, visually handicapped, partially sighted* and, finally, *blind*. Notice I left out obviously demeaning terms, such as *crippled, lame, deaf mute,* and *blind, deaf, and dumb.*

I know that most of the above mentioned terms and phrases were brought about in a sincere effort to accurately define these populations. However, the term *handicap* to many of us implies an inability, or a state of helplessness. As for *handicapper,* that makes me think of someone walking around with a club busting shins.

I happen to be blind. I do not have a problem with phrases such as *visually impaired* or *legally blind.* However, I would like to point out that my vision is not impaired; it is nonexistent. I wonder what my counterparts did before blindness was legalized.

I don't mean to criticize these words and phrases designed to define, but not offend, but in our effort to be *politically correct, we* may be too convoluted.

Recently, I visited Jamaica. While I was engaged in conversation with one of the natives, she suddenly stated, "Oh, your eyes are blind." At first, I wasn't sure what she had said. Then the true meaning of her words hit me, and I smiled and replied, "Yes, they are." The more I think about it, I believe that in her innocent honesty she managed to be more *politically correct* than anyone I have run across.

Prayer of a Dead Beat

Lord, grant me the ability
to wake up and smell the coffee
and let it burn,
the strength to deny reality,
the courage to avoid responsibility,
and the wisdom to pull down the shades
and turn out the lights.

O

I Don't Do Windows

I don't do tiny square panes,
through which the world can be seen
as pretty shapes, colors and words
all carefully designed to make
my machine *user friendly*.
My best choices are not made
by looking at a menu.
My memory is too valuable to be
taken up with icons, gui, or pretty wallpaper.
I don't jump from place to place with
the movement of a curser.
I don't open and close windows
with two basic key strokes.
I don't do numerous reinstallations,
or make calls to the support line.
My world cannot be controlled by mice.

M. J. Lord

To Whom It Should Concern

You may have seen me around,
or maybe you know me. I'm
your student, your neighbor,
or your child's friend. I ride
your bus every day. I deliver
your newspaper. I'm your
baby-sitter or the child that you
care for daily. I'm your patient
or your friend's child. I'm in
your scout troop, church group,
or I'm on your sports team.
Maybe, I'm your niece, nephew,
cousin, or grandchild.

I usually get good grades.
I'm barely passing. My family
has strict religious beliefs. We
never go to church. My parents
have a lot of money, and my
mom is home most of the time.
My parents both work long
hours, and we never seem
to have money. I am an only
child. I have lots of siblings.
I live with my mom and dad.
My mother/father is a single
parent. My parents drink a lot.
My parents never drink.
My family has many friends.
We never go anywhere.
We live in a big house. We live
in subsidized housing.

I'm too fat, or too skinny
My room is always neat.
My room is a mess. I'm
usually shy. I act out
whenever I can. I'm
involved in everything
at school. I don't have
many friends. I cry a lot.
I never cry.

I could be anybody,
or nobody. I think
that I'm nobody, or
at least nobody important.
I've been told often enough
that my feelings and what
I think don't count. I'm
scared a lot. Scared that
something bad is going to
happen, or has already
happened. Scared to go
home, scared not to, and
scared to tell anybody why.

I love my mom and dad, and
I know if I were a better kid,
they'd love me too. I know
that other kids aren't like me.
If I did tell, who would I tell?
Would she believe me, or
would she tell me I'm a bad
kid? Am I bad? I
try to be good.

My parents punish me for
lying. Then, they tell me to

lie to people, maybe even
to you, about how I got my
cuts, bruises, or broken bones.
Sometimes, the names they
call me hurt more than anything
they could do to my body. I'm
afraid to tell anybody what
is happening to me. I do
and I don't want to tell you,
and I'm afraid of what you
might or might not do.

I'm a child, and I'm being
abused by someone at my house.
I need your help.
Please.

M. J. Lord

That Frightened Child

That frightened child
knows nothing of the world today.
She has no sense of time.
She shrinks back
from hateful and loving arms.
Hands shield head and face,
protect against danger.
I wish I could embrace her
and take her to someplace
where objects don't strike,
hands don't hurt,
and words don't scar.

M. J. Lord

Fingerprints

Lines and curves forever ingrained
in flesh leave their marks on
polished glass and shiny metal.
A part of identity unduplicated, unchanged.

No lies are told; no secrets kept.
If examined closely, fingerprints
tell the world where I've been,
and whom and what I've touched.
At times they help me get a job,
make a purchase and show my
hidden innocence or guilt.

Like a polished mirror,
I am stamped by those
who've touched me. I'm
a scrapbook of memories,
each page a special moment.

I'm a road trip to Florida,
Disney World and a sand dollar.
I'm a forbidden mountain climb.
I'm all the people who lived in
cardboard shacks in Tijuana.
I'm Jamaican shops, steel bands,
the musical clang of
slot machines.

I'm all the family crises,
the basement
parties, visits from the ice cream man.
I'm family nights around the television.
I'm fights with my sister Laura.

I'm all the teachers who helped
me make funny symbols into words.
I'm friends and all-night parties.
I'm all my dreams and laughter.
I'm fear and overcoming it.

All these lines and curves leave their mark,
impact, shape, make a difference.

M. J. Lord

Pool of Light

As I open
the drapes
to find
a blazing sky,
sunlight
bathes the room,
covers it like a well-
loved blanket.

Mandy's coat
shines in
its radiance,
as she stretches,
groans and
settles down
to enjoy
the warmth
in canine
bliss.

O

Lilacs

Such sweet aroma.
In my yard in the springtime.
With bright purple bloom.

Storm

We groan as we look
through the spotted window.
I button the collar of my
coat around my neck, and he
snaps open the umbrella. As
we push open the door, a
strong gust of wind throws
us backward, dousing us with
rain and hail. The wind makes
our umbrella sway to and fro,
as we slide and slosh through
puddles. A loud clap of thunder
booms overhead, as we maneuver
between cars and screaming children.

It is a cold dreary day, we
(and the rest of the world) have
decided to go to the mall. I'm
sure that we will never make it to
our car at the far end of the lot.

The umbrella is more of a hinderance
than protection against
bombarding drops of freezing rain.

Breathless, we finally
arrive at the car. As we
climb gratefully inside,
it seems we will never
be dry again. He starts
the engine, turns the heat
on high. The almost
instant blast of hot dusty
air on my face feels wonderful.

The windows fog up from the steam
created by wet clothing and heat.

As I listen to the rhythmic whir, groan, whir,
groan of the windshield wipers,
breathe in the aroma of our
drenched bodies mixed with damp
upholstery, it seems we are completely
alone. That we are literally surrounded
by carloads of people seems
incomprehensible. I giggle, imagining
the two of us making love right there,
while the sounds of the storm, cars
starting up, and people running
fill our ears.

Another loud clap
of thunder booms overhead;
we kiss and smile.

Lori Solymosi
When a Seed Becomes the Sea

5 am Run, Honolulu

Mimosa tree pods
lie on the sidewalk
like sleeping baby snakes.

My silver-ringed fingers
grasp them like forceps
while palm fronds reach
towards varicose clouds.

A crackle and crunch reveal
embryonic seeds sticking
to my perspiring palms.

They will come to life later
in some chosen art form.
Like a seed traveling on

the wind, my ideas take flight
to the most unexpected places.
A seed will become the sea,
a twig become a tree trunk
in the collage, in which
I'll wrap a cord as a border.

Panting, I push the pods
into swollen red pockets
of my damp running shorts.

Satisfied with my labor,
I resume my emergence
into morning.

"Birthday," Collograph by Lori Solymosi, 1996.

Red Licorice

Today I bought a package
of cherry red shoe lace licorice.
I ate the whole thing,
twirled it around my fingers
and tied it in bows, let it snake
down my chest and coil around my tongue.

I felt as evil as Eve.
There it was, in the check-out-aisle-
Eden, among the other temptations.
There were nail clippers, playing cards,
key chains and pine tree-shaped
air fresheners, but it was
the color red that attracted me.
Shiny as an apple. Corn syrup, sugar,
red dye, 140 calories per serving.
Nutritional value: none.

I was six again and wanted
the *red* one. The *red* crayon,
the *red* balloon, the *red* Life Saver.
When I was a child, we never even
thought about asking for candy
at the grocery store check-out.
It was forbidden.

But tonight, I think
I'll stay up as late as I can,
go to bed with my clothes on,
and maybe not even wash
my hands or face.

Lori Solymosi

Shimmering Silver

Slashing the stem of the ailing
jade plant with a silver razor,
I feel the sticky sap run over
my fingers. The silver knife
blade looks inviting, yet
forbidding. I have always loved
the cool shimmer of silver,
the hot hue of summer.

I remember Karen and me running
around with our BatMan beach towel
capes; we collected silver Juicy Fruit
gum wrappers. Mouths full of minty
wads, we sat in the hot sand. Our
wet hair smelled of salt.

We wove yards of gum wrapper
chains. Our eyes squinted from
reflections dancing on waves.
There was magic in those zigzags.
The longer they got, the more
powerful we felt.

All summer, I cut stems, dug them
into dirt-filled Dixie cups set in
silver pie pans. They lined every
window sill. Impatiens, begonias,
kaleidoscope coleus propagated,
multiplied, nurtured.

As a child, I loved to touch,
collect things, stick fingers into
sugar-white icing on the gala
graduation cake, squeeze red

berries on the driveway bushes.
I smashed slimy snails stuck
to slippery rocks or yanked them
off and watched them suck air.
Silvery Fourth of July sparklers
seared my fingers.

Curiosity led me up the ladder
to the shiny paint scraper.
I was warned, but like a fish
attracted to a shimmering lure,
I took the bait. I was fascinated
when the silver blade penetrated
my flesh so effortlessly. My warm
blood flowed beautifully until
the pain came. Now

I collect silver bracelets when
I travel. Some are gifts, some
symbols of success I wear like
shiny memories. I like the cool
shimmer of silver and the hot hue
of summer.

I like to shine my silver.
I've tried pink pasty creams
and sulfur-smelling liquids
that promise to clean in seconds
but take my breath away. I still
prefer to polish my silver by hand.
I like to feel the ridges, twists,
smooth cuffs, and zigzag chains.

Lori Solymosi

Baby Marcus

Nestled in a soft, lamb's ear hammock, he is
secured like a sprouting stem to a trellis.

The newborn's arms reach out like vines,
searching for something to grasp.
Needing to be nurtured and fed,
tiny roots tap dance in the dirt.

He's cozy in early summer grass,
his hair like dew, skin like cotton.

With a breeze, flows a scent—
the scent of innocence.

"Baby Marcus," Aqueous Medium, Lori Solymosi, 1995.

Lori Solymosi

Contemplating Their Arrival

A woman sits on the sun-faded sofa,
contemplating their arrival.
It has been months since she last saw them.
Her memory is like the yellowed photograph,
small hands reaching up to theirs,
taking her first steps.
Her parents' faces, young and scrubbed,
are like shiny fresh red apples
picked for their beauty,
wax-coated for protection.

Scanning the picture-perfect room,
she focuses on the dead grape ivy leaves,
upon the pastel foyer slate.
She forgot to sweep.
It always feels like there is something
left undone. Never enough time to prepare.
Like the time she was still packing toys
and her family left for a picnic.
Alone and afraid, she hid behind
the plump, chintz armchair,
sobbing.

She looks down at the list of
Things to Do when Mom and Dad Visit
and realizes that her hands look
just like Mom's did
when she was this age. Those
hands would be there after school
holding a teacup and *Reader's Digest*.

It is a quarter past three; her
parents should have been here by now.
The kettle whistles and she bolts.
Her hands fumble and steam scorches,

leaving her knuckles red.
What if they got lost?
She shouldn't have let them drive.
When she was seventeen, she drove
her boyfriend's red Sport Spyder
into New Haven and got lost
in a web of one-way streets.
She remembers pulling over afraid
and sobbing.

When the rusted station wagon
with the out-of-state plates appears,
she is relieved.
Running out to greet them, she notices
Dad's hair seems grayer, his stride a little slower.
Mom reaches up her arms;
red, arthritic knuckles
extend for a hug.
She feels her mother's fragile bones
and sees her own reflection in
prescription sunglasses, blurred.
She is afraid and bites her lip
to keep from sobbing.

Lori Solymosi

La Bella Vista Estate Sale

Dedicated to the anonymous grandmother with respect and gratitude.

Following lipstick red arrows,
I pass powder-pale residents
wandering empty halls,

enter the once forbidden
cloister— a lifetime reduced to
a one-bedroom apartment.

I peruse piles of crocheted
pillows, potpourri in lavender
nylon net, paint-by-number
oils, and dusty bric-a-brac.

A motorized wheelchair sits
lonely in the parlor corner.
Clothes placed on the death bed,
like faded leaves fallen from a
withered oak, are still fresh
with the scent of Jean Naté.

Children sit, blank as the wall
where the family portrait
once hung. Empty like the 50th
anniversary crystal vase.

Someone's elbow nudges me;
I fill a bag with lost memories
marked down from a quarter
to fifteen cents.

I don't even offer my condolences.

Lori Solymosi

Amish Quilt

In Lancaster, Pennsylvania,
I admire the quilts,
hung like laundry
outside shops.
Inside they are draped
like newspapers
at a library; I browse.

Even if I could afford
one of these gems,
I could never choose.

I try to organize my life
like a perfect Amish quilt,
no discordant colors.
I balance my proteins
and fats, match the
patterns and textures of
activities— 24 hours to a day,
12 stitches to an inch.

I prewash my appointments
and baste together relationships.
I trace my mistakes and cut
the superfluous.
I piece together torn
dreams and sew.

But still my seams
are not perfect. The
quilt pattern of my life
is a crazy one.

Lori Solymosi

The Magic Secret

My nine-year-old daughter
often wishes life could be
a video tape—
rewound, fast forwarded,
erased at will.

If only life could be
a magic trick.
How many of us would choose
to live in Disneyland, Narnia or Oz?

Is the hand quicker than the eye?
Just yesterday, I was watching
Fantasia and eating Nonpareils
shaped like tiny mushroom caps,
which sprout like my daughter's growth.

I have a secret
place inside myself
where innocence still lives.
I can be the sorcerer's apprentice,
grab the magic wand, don the
black top hat and cape,
set white doves free.

My daughter and I,
collect shells on the beach,
play tag with the waves,
go down a slide and feel
the salty wind braid our
tangled hair.

In a flutter of a wand,
she will be married,
the white doves of childhood
a remembrance.

When the responsibilities of
adulthood arrive, she'll
remember this tiny secret:

Life is like a video tape.
Although we cannot rewind,
fast forward or erase,
we do have the power
to pause.

Lori Solymosi

The Waiting Tank

Waiting outside my therapist's office,
I stare at the tropical fish.
I am tired and would like to sleep, like
Ophelia, caressed in a cover of warm water
amongst the algae, my hair flowing with seaweed.

There is unseen life in a tide pool,
invisible to the naked eye, yet present.

Tropical fish, were they born in captivity
or taken from their paradise for our pleasure?
Were they captured for our captivation

to have their eyes gouged out by a predator
or to suffer for their sins like Oedipus Rex?
The pretty one is dead and floats buoyantly,
mouth open but unable to suck.

Black with white spots, she will be skimmed off
and discarded, most likely in the sewer.

The sound of the fish tank filter is constant.
As my thoughts wander, it becomes
a monotonous drone.

Fish come and fish go; there is always
another, eager to be fed.

Lori Solymosi

The Trapeze Artist

She flies through the air with the greatest of ease,
the daring young gal on the flying trapeze.

Climbing the elongated
ladder to the trapeze,
I wonder if this will be
the time I plunge.
Exhilaration warms my body.
My thighs tremble;
my palms perspire.

I must go higher, exceed
my last performance. I swing,
fly, flirt with danger.

This freedom I feel
exceeds any other.
Alone, I soar
toward the sun.
How close can I get
without singeing my wings?

I was born into this circus.
Looking down I see three rings.
I want to take them all in,
concentrate on the swing.
My timing must be precise.
Clowns, elephants, lions
roar for my attention.

I look ahead and see
my partner's hands reach out.
Now, he says.

Startled, I let go and
trust him with my body,
my mind.

Lori Solymosi

Dream Flight

Flanked by four pine posters,
I lay my tired body down,
before I drift off to slumber.
My mind takes its usual flight,
entering a Chagall painting. I
float *Over the Town*.

Crimson, cadmium, and cobalt
paint streaks across the
indigo sky, faster than a 747
in my thoughts.

Fate brought us together
from another continent and generation.
We were Cupid and Psyche. I placed
you on a marble pedestal, as if you were
a Greek god.

I was like Mt. Fuji, a live volcano
ready to erupt, burst forth into
destruction.

You were like a wave of warm water,
calming my internal fire,
yet igniting my soul.

Our first day together, we wandered
through glass gardens filled with orchids.
The antique pipe organ resounding
and your hand in mine sent tremors
echoing through my body.

Bach, the smell of autumn, and hundreds
of mums created a sensual tapestry.
Your leather jacket, cool
against my face, your *Pierre Cardin*

and *True Green* aroma engulfed me.

My world changed that November day
fifteen years ago. I knew I could never
go back. Pills and powders paled compared
to the high I felt from you.

Looking back on our travels. I wonder
Was it all a dream flight?

The summer in Europe with the
indoor Parisian picnic, we feasted
on baguettes, fleshy ripe tomatoes
and cheese. Wet hair and *Dom Pérignon*
dripped on my pin-striped nightshirt, as
the sun set behind the Eiffel Tower.

You showed me where you swam
across the blue Danube as
a child. Castles, museums and
cathedrals were our amusement park.

On and on as I reminisce, images and
sounds fill me. Like Mona Lisa's smile,
the portrait of my past comes alive.

Now here in Michigan, I think of you
climbing Mt. Miyajima alone.
It is hard to remember when the
ambrosia turned to sour milk.

These days, I travel alone in my
imagination, white paper my vehicle.
Pills and powders tempt me. New
mythological Gods entice me with
their idealized personae, white
marble limbs, chiseled features
and fresh new idioms.

Read the Signs

1.
I read the signs,
warning signs:
HIGH VOLTAGE
MEN AT WORK

The parishioners greet me,
shake my hand,
and pray for me.

CLOSED
NO TRESPASSING
KEEP OUT

The pastor visits my home.
He calls me sister,
But you can't teach my children,
he says smiling.
I read the signs,
warning signs:
ONE WAY ONLY
EXIT

The choir rejoices,
Everyone is welcome.
There's a home right
here for you . . . if you
sign this covenant.

STOP

I read the signs,
warning signs:
THE ICE IS UNSAFE

2.
You say you understand me,
hold my hand and hug me.
You hang my picture on your wall.

BEWARE, ROAD NARROWS AHEAD
YOU MUST TURN RIGHT
YOU MUST TURN LEFT

You call me friend.
You call me long distance.
Suddenly you tell me
I've overstepped the boundaries.
You should have
worn a sign.

I read the signs,
warning signs.
Now you want to
change your story.

Lori Solymosi

Fruits of My Labor

I preserve my past
like cucumbers in brine,
chilies in sherry and
watermelon rind. I sow,
harvest and prepare.

Some memories are sour
cherries, some bitter herbs:
abortions, miscarriages,
all the lost children.

The labels and dates fade.
Jars are neatly lined in rows
in a cool, dry place
untouched for years.

Away in my cellar,
the dust grows thick.
I discover the seals
are not secure, the
pectin has a crack.

Blood red berries
ooze to the floor,
seep and stain my mind,
grow enzymes. Odorless,
colorless, tasteless, I am
poisoned by my own fruit.

Bodies of my unborn children
float in formaldehyde,
among the spilled preserves,
and send me running.

Upstairs, I face my past,
drop my stained body
into a milk bath, let the
water purify me.
I feel my memories
ladle off, my grief
strain through a sieve.

Pulling Up Roots

Like the red hot peppers
hanging on my kitchen wall,
I felt every drop of joy
wrung out of me. A
year ago, I left my home.
Dried up, my thoughts
rattled like seeds inside
the brittle red shell.

It wasn't a coincidence
we met, dear friend.
Like a wooden cross
supports a scarecrow,
we held each other up.

Black crows flew across
a streaked Michigan sky,
that heard our secrets.
We walked miles, trailing
four seasons and gaining
power with each step.

We laughed and cried,
stretched mind and body,
stomped through the anger
mud and slush: my marriage,
your divorce. We crossed
the same bridge day after day,
but we always saw new water.

Now my life flourishes,
and you are the one leaving
to plant new seeds where
it is warm and the sun
shines year round. I would
grieve if I weren't so
happy for you. I think of you
as I prepare the garden
for winter. My chapped hands
pulling up roots, I see you
as the hardiest of sunflowers,
sturdy stalk withstanding extremes,
face still turned towards the light.

"Raise Your Hands," Collograph, Lori Solymosi, 1996

Lori Solymosi

Indian Summer

Leaves fall like tears,
staining white summer cement.

Gray clouds roll in;
hurricanes destroy

homes, leave lives bare,
as the linden tree

outside my window.
Falling apart is my life.

What was planted in spring
dies in the autumn frost.

I hold lifeless plants,
my puppy's lifeless paw.

A dreaded phone call comes;
this time it's from Mom.

The distance ties my hands,
the telephone call chills,

like wind beating
against pain.

Perhaps if I bury them,
tulips will give me hope.

Karen Renaud
Beyond Stillness

Beyond Stillness

Poised among goldenrod and roses,
knowledge just behind the din,
I sift through boldly golden petals,
loosen dreams adrift warm wind.

Truths lie emphatically in silence
and solid oak, soft-muted stone.
Stillness captures, envelops answers;
essentially, I search alone.

I walk within my world to notice
sunflowers guided by the sun,
hawks that cruise to catch soft currents,
deer that choose which paths to run.

Listen to whispers between tall branches,
wait for wisdom in hoot-owl's call.
Absolutes live in every-day moments—
answers exist within us all.

Pushing Up the Screen

Laura lets her blue eyes go blank. Tucking into herself, she prays her teacher's glance will pass her by. Her parents' thunderous argument, last night, makes it impossible to concentrate on long division today.

Later, the quiet child with a no-nonsense haircut hangs around the school building until the last of her friends leave. Not wanting to go home, she hopes to be invited to someone's house. She starts walking, wondering where to go. Avoiding everyone's eyes, Laura succeeds in blending in with her surroundings. No one takes notice of her until a neighborhood brat named Rod comes by. Rod loves to taunt Laura. Sensing her fragile nature, he takes full advantage. Today is no different; with a grin and a stick smeared with gooey black stuff, Rod approaches Laura. Knowing that he is faster than she, Laura tries to put on a brave face. Rod just laughs, runs the blackened stick across Laura's blouse and skirt. He walks away. Laura's eyes puddle with tears.

Slowly, Laura heads for home. The sidewalk in front of her seems alive. The wind is playing with sun reflections by making tree branches prance. The shadows elongate everything. Laura stops next to a simple, slight tree. She smiles when she sees that both she and the tree send out long strong silhouettes.

Entering her house quietly, she tries sneaking up the stairs. Barbara hears her. "Where have you been? It's time to vacuum!" Barbara chides her younger sister. "What happened to my skirt?"

"Please don't tell Dad; Rod did it!" Laura pleads.

"That was my favorite skirt! Then Mom made me give it to Ellie, and now you've taken it, and you've ruined it! You are really going to get it!" Barbara yells.

Miserably, Laura closes herself in her room to change. She stuffs the blouse and skirt into the back of a lower drawer, hoping she'll get away with something this time. She finds solace with Goldie, loves the feel of the bird's feathers, soft against her cheek. She still can't believe that her mother had let her keep the parakeet. Their family has never had a pet. She knows that she only has Goldie because the bird was a birthday gift from her friend Sarah. Laura is well aware of the fact that Sarah's father is one of her parents' best customers. Laura loves Goldie. She feels that, to Goldie, she matters.

After vacuuming, Laura sneaks out of the house and heads for the nearby shopping center. A group of kids is hanging out. At last, Laura can relax. She joins in the crowd, talking, laughing, feeling free.

Before she realizes it, it's late. If she doesn't help Ellie make dinner, she will be in for it. As she rushes home, she becomes more and more concerned. She is really late. Her stomach sinks when she sees her mother's Mercedes. At least her father's car isn't in the garage, yet.

Finding her mother in better humor than usual, Laura quickly sets the table and starts making a salad. "Mom," she speaks hesitantly, "I wish you were here when I come home from school. Barbara always yells at me." Laura knows she should stop talking, but continues. "When Sarah gets home from school, her mom is always there. They have a snack and talk about their day."

Laura's mother jumps up, knocking her stool backwards. Laura flinches, frozen in place. Her mother's eyes, magnified behind thick glasses, have a crazed glare. She grabs Laura by the shoulders.

"You selfish little bitch; all you care about is yourself! It's hard enough without you causing problems." She lets go of Laura so quickly that Laura falls to the floor.

The young girl finishes making the salad, runs to her room. Opening Goldie's cage, she hums softly as she holds the bird close to her cheek. Gradually, Laura's breathing calms.

Throughout dinner, Laura almost doesn't dare to breathe. She wills herself invisible. Then it happens.

"Laura ruined my favorite skirt," Barbara starts. "She got tar all over it!"

"It wasn't my fault . . . ."

Her father's mood darkens immediately. "It's never your fault, is it? How many times do I have to tell you not to play in your good clothes?"

"That brat is always causing trouble. She made me so mad before dinner that I can hardly eat," Laura's mother throws her napkin down over her almost empty plate. "I've had such a hard day!"

Laura finds herself being pulled to her feet and dragged down the basement stairs. There, Laura's father grabs a piece of lumber and starts spanking her with it.

"Your mother and I have enough trouble with our damned customers; we don't need this when we get home!" He hits her even harder.

When her father finally winds down, Laura painfully climbs two flights of stairs to her room. She can hear her younger sister snickering, and Barbara ordering her to come do the dishes.

Closing her bedroom door, Laura gingerly sits down on her bed. She opens Goldie's cage and coaxes the bird onto her finger.

"You're the only one who cares about me, Goldie." Laura's tears run down her cheeks.

Suddenly, her father bursts into the room.

"If you ever upset your mother again, you are going to get the beating of your life. Now put that damn bird away, before I do it for you. Get downstairs and do the dishes. You can do Barbara's chores, too, for ruining her good skirt!" With a slam of the door, he's gone.

Laura sits perfectly still, pets her cherished friend. She stops crying. Slowly, she opens her bedroom window. Then, more determinedly, she pushes up the screen. She inches her finger that supports Goldie out through the opening. Gently, she tickles Goldie's tail feathers. Smiling through her tears, Laura releases the bird.

"Pushing Up the Screen" is an excerpt from a novel-in-progress.

Karen Renaud

At the Well

I come for just a sip.
Your push
takes me by surprise.
I fall so quickly, down this well—
wanting, still, to believe
that you would never push me.

Layer upon layer
of jagged rocks jut out,
tear at my skin.
I hit icy water, shocked
at the strength
of my own illusions.

Guardedly, I start my ascent,
use those sharp rocks
to gain footing,
grapple with my lessons.

Out of the abyss, in fresh air,
I continue my journey.
You are busy, pushing still,
fearful of your own descent.

Karen Renaud

In Spite of Everything

I am here to seek,
to perceive, to receive others.
We are not discordant drops
adrift upon a despondent sea.
Our lives converge, merge
into a uni-verse.

I am here
to make a difference.
Not a huge
save-the-world difference,
rather a significant
one-to-one difference.
Within interactions
my true spirit is realized.

I am here, struggling,
not to strike back
at those who have broken trust.
This is my disquieting quest.

I am judged,
will be judged,
should judge myself,
by the esteem I gift to others.
Everything I give —
from selfish to sublime —
releases,
rebounds,
reciprocates,

reveals who I am.

Resolution and Good Intentions

"Humph!" Stefen didn't mean to "humph," it just slipped out. Every time he saw those two, irritation set in. They sure didn't feel like family, yet everyone acted like they belonged here, in his house!

In all of his 78 years, Stefan had never had a problem like this one! All he wanted was a peaceful, normal retirement. How dare Kate dilute his family by bringing these . . . these . . . urchins into their lives! She, with children of her own already! David and Patrick were sturdy blue-eyed boys who showed off the proud Slovak stock they came from. He shouldn't be surprised that Kate would do this. She was his one grandchild who never easily fell into place.

His wife brought him a large drink and gently shooed the children away from his chair. He calmed down a bit; Mother always made his drinks just right. He wondered how she could so easily accept these children as part of the family. At least, he thought, we have eight real great-grandchildren. But what would his friends think if they saw these two? What would they say if they knew?

For months now, he had been trying to get used to Kate's new children. He loved Kate, even admired her resolution and good intentions. But why did she always have to try to save the whole world? Why couldn't she just leave well-enough alone?

"Grandpa," Kate came over and sat on the arm of his chair, seeming to have read his thoughts, "we need to talk about Jin Soon and Jae Lee. I know how hard it is for you to understand why Mike and I decided to adopt. It's also hard for you to get used to great-grandchildren who look so different. We thought long and hard about this, Grandpa; we really wanted those two to be ours."

"But, Katie, you could have had more kids of your own!" As head of the family, he had to make her understand! "Why did you do this? Why did you have to change things?"

"Grandpa, think about it. Children are one of our best legacies of life. How they become ours is irrelevant; they soon grow to be their own persons. Mike and I love all of our kids completely, with no difference between feelings for Dave, Pat, Jinni, or Jae. Please grow to accept them, Gramps; you are so important to us!"

Kate walked over to the children, protectively wrapped her arms around Jae and Jin Soon. Stefen saw maternal concern and love radiate from her eyes.

Weeks went by between visits. Stefan tried to adjust to the idea of his new great-grandchildren. He'd even shown a picture of Kate's family to one of his friends. He had been strangely disappointed, however, when George hadn't seemed upset by the newest additions. Didn't anyone share his confusion?

Christmas Eve came, finding Stefan in great spirits. His whole family was coming over. Mother had been up since five o'clock, cooking, polishing, and wrapping. Snow had fallen, and everyone was expected soon.

Kate's family was one of the first to arrive. After greetings, Kate went into the kitchen to help her grandmother. Stefan watched the younger children swoop down around the tree, looking at the presents. Jin Soon was showing Jae Lee how to locate the gifts that were his. Stefan's eyes wandered around the festive room, coming to rest on the nativity scene, which sat on a low table next to the tree. The tree's blinking bulbs reflected on the tranquil faces of the figurines, illuminating them. Stefen watched as Mary, Joseph, and baby Jesus changed to red, to yellow, then darker, then back to white.

The house started to fill with family and holiday cheer. The women and older girls were helping in the kitchen; the older boys had been rounded up by their fathers to bring up the folding tables and chairs from the basement. The doorbell rang. Stefan, expecting more family, opened the door to two of his neighborhood pals, Doug and Bob. The men seemed to startle as they entered the living room and saw Jin Soon and Jae Lee.

"What —" Doug started.

Stefan interrupted his friend. "Doug, Bob, I'd like you to meet Kate's youngest two. Jinni, Jae, come here a minute."

The children shyly walked over to the men. In a quiet little voice, Jin Soon greeted Doug and Bob, "Nice to meet you, Sirs." She and Jae Lee smiled. Stefan couldn't help but be a little proud of how polite the children were, and of how well Jinni was learning English. He sent the children into the kitchen to ask their great-grandmother to bring in drinks for the men.

"My God!" Bob said, when the children were out of sight, "What are those — ?"

"Those children are ours." The men turned to see Mike and his older boys enter the room. "They're the newest additions to our family."

Stefan's neighbors looked uncomfortable. "Look, Steve," Doug said, after a pause, "we can't stay. Only came to wish you a merry Christmas."

"Well, thanks, guys." Stefan also looked uneasy. He stepped out onto the porch with the men as they left.

"Ha!" Bob waited for Stefan to close the door before speaking. "Looks like the family's complexion has changed a bit, eh, Steve? You poor slob, having to put up with something like that! Why don't you just tell Kate to leave those, those —?"

Stefan interrupted Bob, surprising himself with his reply. "Those children, they're my granddaughter Kate's kids. Those children, why, they're my great-grandchildren, Bob. Merry Christmas to you both." Stefan ended the conversation by stepping inside and closing the door.

Entering the house to the sound of Christmas hymns, the proud old man slowly walked over to his chair, listened as his family sang "Silent Night."

When the singing ended, Jae Lee walked tentatively towards Stefan. "Gate Gampa," the little boy's voice was barely audible, "peasant for you." Jae stood an arm's length away from Stefan's chair, a childishly-wrapped present in his hand.

Stefan felt a swelling in his chest and found he had to clear a lump from his throat before he could respond.

This story is dedicated to Julia and John Wozarik, who welcomed all of their new great-grandchildren with open arms.

Karen Renaud

Entwined

Split from mother plants, Jim and I graft
scion to stem, rejuvenate in moist fertile soil,
establish our own hybrid stock. Buds burst forth.

Readily, the first twig quick-forms.
Early top-growth. Soon, another lateral
sprig appears. We water, nurture. Roots
anchor, firm. Our crown is not yet full.

Grafting two delicate buds of strong stock,
we enhance our leafed canopy. Inner cambium
layers of soft cellular tissue enjoin. Snug
bonds secure new sprouts to our parent tree.

Soon, first-grown branches off-shoot;
roots entwine with those of nearby trees.
Tendrils unite. These fresh saplings flourish.

Our family arbor grows graceful, bark-solid,
resists winds, freezes, and thaws.
Points of attachment interweave.
Sun shines. Showers quench.
Our ever-expanding canopy, for now,
is complete. Several varieties of the same
fruit grow on our family tree.

Wedding Ring

Sparkle of hope, it starts:
Young, with early babies
and empty accounts.
Its shimmer brightens our struggles.

Beacon of light, it becomes:
Partners, busy with children
and life's business.
Its beam illuminates our paths.

Radiance of passion, it gleams:
Together, all alone
with midnight swims.
Its flame reflects our everyday moments.

Brilliance of diamond, it is:
Wiser, always growing —
after twenty-five years.
Its sparkle still dazzles our lives.

Karen Renaud

Rushwind Call

I walk along, my steps almost silent.
Movement. Deer.
We appraise each other.
Doe startles, stamps her right front hoof,
sends vibrations of notice.

Her children, prancing under a willow branch, tense.
Their expressions mirror Doe's:
alert, poised, composed.

Young mother stretches her neck.
Nostrils search the breeze for scent.
Our eyes link.

I, the intruder, acquiesce.
Avert my eyes.
Bow my head.
Soon my peaceful will is sensed.
She lowers the flag.
Relaxes her stance.

A sudden SNAP
prompts swift retreat. Doe's and babies' tails white!
Wishing trust, I hear defeat.
Rushwind call
her warning cry.

Mid-leap, it seems,
Doe pauses,
turns and looks my way.
Our spirits connect.

Then she is gone.

Karen Renaud

Renewal

The rain descends, nestles
in awaiting arrays of green.

Not able to sleep, visions of poems
sink before they're secured.

Releasing my sensibilities, I run
to the downpour, let it flow. Free.

Could I have saved you;
could you have saved yourself?

Tears fall, I can't catch my breath,
my vision is bruised from within.

You died so recently, I can't write, can't
think, get back inside myself, yet a

robin still prances in the sunrise shower,
delighted in her earthly bounty.

Softly Cries Rain

"No, I haven't seen her in three weeks. Pour me another, Stan." Dan pushes his glass towards the bartender, looks back at Tim. "This time I thought she was going to stay awhile . . . . Thanks, Stan; you're there when I need you, buddy."

Dan and Tim gaze upon the vaguely opaque window-front, watch raindrops merge in small rivulets that rush toward the bottom of the glass. Tim watches their paths converge. Dan notices one perfect teardrop going its own way.

"I heard her play, once." Tim taps his fingers in time to the blues playing over the bar's speakers. "At Alvin's Finer Delicatessen last winter. She's really good."

"It's her voice that got me. Sweet silk, with a touch of whiskey. That's where I met her, too. At Alvin's."

"Really? I thought you've known her a long time."

"I have, but we didn't get close 'til last Valentine's Day." Dan's voice hardens. "I guess you can say we're close."

"You're still together, aren't you? If not, there's a lot of guys who would like to . . . . "

Dan interrupts with a laugh; he doesn't sound happy. He unloads on his friend, laments about Cassi's new partner. Ken plays harmonica to Cassi's guitar. "They're together, practicing, all the time. A 'platonic' relationship she says. Cassi has many relationships, but always keeps her distance."

"Man, I couldn't take that!"

"It's not as bad as I make it sound; she never goes too far. And when Cassi's with me, it's crystal clear that we're meant to be together. Cassi has a way of loving, really being there, grabbing and holding every moment. She's like a high that I've just gotta have."

Later, at home, Dan turns on the radio. He remembers the first time he held Cassi. The silky feel of her thick black curls. That night, he had felt her longing. It was in the way she held her arms so tightly around his neck. As if she would never let go. But when they kissed, he saw fear in her revealing eyes. She turned and left him then. Didn't say a word.

The phone rings. It's Cassi's sister, Debby, wanting to know if he's heard from her.

"I don't know if I ever will again. I think I've scared her off for good this time."

"Come on, Dan. We've all been through this before. She's probably on a tour that she didn't tell us about. With Ken."

"Yeah, with Ken."

"Mom's worried; she hasn't heard from her in quite a while, longer than usual."

Dan ends the conversation, promises to call around and try to locate Cassi. He appreciates having Debby's call as an excuse for trying to find her.

From his radio, he hears Bonnie Raitt sing:

> *She gives herself to him;*
> *but he's still on the outside.*
> *She's alone in this world.*
> *She's nobody's girl . . .*

Knowing he shouldn't, Dan pours himself another drink.

He pictures the way Cassi's hazel eyes warmed the first time he saw them fill with love. They were sitting right here, in Dan's living room, having a picnic in front of the fireplace. Cassi's ebony hair was highlighted from the flames' incandescence. She had made them a special Valentine's dinner, linguine and biscuits. Dan turned on their favorite radio program; jazz eased into the room. Pouring Cassi a glass of wine, he listened as she spoke of her childhood.

"So, after Dad died, Mom would just disappear, sometimes for weeks. Oh, she always had some excuse, but I knew she was with other men. Grandma Jenkins was always good to me, but I missed Dad so much. I couldn't understand how he could leave us like that . . . I was too young to understand death. I swore nobody would leave me that way again. It hurt too much. I used to get so mad at Mom, think she didn't care about me and Dad and Debby. I know now that she was just running from her own devils. But I didn't know that back then."

"You must have been so lonely."

"It wasn't too bad." A whisp of a laugh came from deep inside her throat. "I used to play in the backyard, in the white lilac bushes against our house. They were my refuge. I had an old ukulele that belonged to Dad. I'd bring my dolls and some blankets and one of my Mom's angora sweaters. I'd stay behind those bushes for hours, imagining myself in front of a crowd, singing. Everybody loved me. Everybody wanted me. I think I spent half my childhood hidden behind those bushes. I can still feel the way Mom's sweaters felt against my skin." She reached over to Dan, then, eyes intimate. "I never wanted to settle down before, Dan. You make me want to do just that."

Dan was used to Cassi's escapes, but this time he was worried. He hoped she wouldn't go too far. He thought of all the men in her life. The ones who go to her concerts. All the other musicians. The agents always trying to sign her. Don't they realize that Cassi can't be signed, can't be committed to a contract, a long-term gig, a single man? One day, though, Dan knew that she would be all his. She had promised him, that night, in front of the fire.

"Someday, you and I will have a little Danny and a little Cassi to tend to; we'll be a real family. It will be so great." Cassi's eyes never lied to Dan.

Dan's calls are futile. Failing to find anyone who knows Cassi's whereabouts, he dials Debby's number.

"Sorry to call back so late, Debby. I've tried everywhere; I can't find Cassi."

"That's OK, Dan. You know, you're the best thing that's ever happened to Cassi. I wish she'd realize that."

"Thanks, Debby, that means a lot. Someday she'll discover that she really needs me."

"She's never needed anyone, Dan. It's always been just her and her guitar." Debby pauses. "Actually, she's a walking contradiction. Inside, she cries for what she needs. She'd find it, if she just stopped running."

Dan hangs up the phone, winces at the memory of the last time he held Cassi. He hadn't meant to blurt it out, but he had suddenly had this great vision of a Valentine's Day wedding. Things had been going so well; she had just told him that she was planning to stay for a while. The proposal had just slipped out, like a yawn that refused to be stifled.

Immediately, Cassi's eyes sparked; the bolt smacked him, hard. "Dan, please. What the hell did you do that for?"

She left him then.

A delicate ivory bird floats through a cloud, seemingly at arm's length. He reaches; she's farther than he thought. Thrown off balance, he falls. She flies on, feathers glistening. A cloud softly cries rain. A bell chimes.

Coming into wakefulness, Dan realizes that his doorbell has been ringing for some time.

Sprinting to the front door, Dan impatiently pulls it open, hoping, at last, it will be her.

Karen Renaud

Life in the Music

for Karl

1 . . . 2 . . . 3. . . 4 . . . Howlin' Wolf speaks of life
to Eric Clapton, as he teaches him the blues.
Ain't got nothin' to do but count off, then change.
He tells Steve Winwood, *Drop in on the boom.*
Twang of the wang dang doodle hits internal chord,
the key to the highway down life's hazy road.

Robert Johnson suffers the crossroad.
His music transcends his short stark life
to speak to others, to strike a chord
in all who take time to know the blues.
Chester Burnett sings in a voice that booms
about the hoodoo man, and the many changes

we all go through, as we allow those changes
to open us up to all that is down our road.
The *wooo-wooo-wooo,* the thunderous boom
is part of our days, part of our lives.
The good times, the bad, the times of the blues.
The times we hold on by a fine fragile cord.

Screaming slide guitar, delicate balance of chords
dance up the fretboard, explode, then change
to mellow down easy to the good moanin' blues
which run in muddy waters, travel country roads,
speak of your life, of my life, of all life,
with the rhythm, and the blues, and the boom.

Don't ever come back, your dad's voice, a sonic boom,
rips you from the womb, cuts an umbilical cord,
shoots you to the world, releases you to life.
Uplifted by your music, you survive the painful change,
pull yourself in place, travel your own road,
learn to trust again, empowered by the blues.

The sound is a river, Santana speaks of the blues,
to take you to the last day of life, when, **boom**,
you'll hear heaven-bound music at the end of earth's road.
Stevie Ray, Albert King, and Howlin' crankin' out chords
to be your balm to calm through eternal change,
as sweet little angels spread joy to all celestial life.

So, wander this meandering road, watching internal chords
of black, of white, of blue. You'll hear your personal boom
signal change. Explore, soar, glory in your immortal life.

Karen Renaud

Bad Planning

I could have afforded
that flannel-lined jacket,
coveted the scarlet
swing-coat instead.
I planned the purchase
with next week's check.

But now that check, gone
before it's come:
unexpected bills to pay.
Snow storms,
I fend the cold
in my old blue sweater,

listen to my teeth chatter.

Karen Renaud

Surrender the Fall

Pondering reflections
upon a summer pool, my gaze
echoes from its shimmering surface.
Cooling winds alter mirrored clouds.
My image startles my perception.
I acknowledge the weight of the seasons
upon my once resilient body.

Slipping into silky depths, I float.
The ripples tickle. Refresh. Energize.
I glide in glistening weightlessness.
Buoyancy lifts my spirit.

Wrapped in warmth, I savor
one last summer swim.
Entering the autumn of my years,
I am not fooled by fall,
not mesmerized by its dazzle.
Soon, autumn will fall to barren winter.

Bubbles burst through water's shroud,
expose my body to chilling winds.
A squirrel hides hickory nuts,
prepares for winter's austerity.
Immersed too long, the warm water
puckers my skin. It is time to relinquish
my sanctuary, surrender to the changing.
Reluctantly, I emerge from my familiar haven.

The invigorating air smells faintly sweet.
Brilliant autumn leaves highlight a sapphire sky.
I watch a goldfinch alight from the treetop,
catch the breeze, and soar.

Karen Renaud

The Answer

I struggle with questions every day,
why people do the things they do.

It's clear how we should all behave
to be remembered when we are through.

Everyone seems to be closed-minded
to what is so easy for me to see.

Our world would improve if everyone stopped
being themselves, and acted like me!

Anita Elaine Page
Mending Circumstances

Between Lies Truth

Seagreen waters wash over us,
as waves from Orpheus' lyre
call us to the land of the living.
We stand naked in our passions
and dance to the music of poetry,
in love, bonding to each other,
still not knowing ourselves.

Anita Elaine Page

Playing on Key

One leaf hangs on a moist branch,
on a bough, on a trunk of tree
that stands strong and silent
on December's last day.

It is still and silvery
like a sheathed sword.
Ice crystals form.
Sparkling snow catches its breath,
pauses to winter's tunes,

sings with bending winds,
whistles soft notes.
The bronze leaf twirls and
gently flutters in time
to a distant beating of drums.

The Chocolate Easter Bunny

Emily looked at the chocolate bunny crouched on the top of the three drawer, oak dresser crowded in the small room. There was barely enough space to squeeze between it and the iron double bed. The attached mirror reflected a bare dingy wall and the milk chocolate Easter bunny. It was without a wrapper, deliciously softened from the heat reflecting out of the hot air register from the coal furnace.

The tempting odor floated delicately toward Emily's six-year-old nose. She had deliberately walked past it now for one week and two whole days. Chocolate scent flooded her senses as the bunny sat staring at her loneliness. Its eyes were inviting Emily to taste the sweetness of belonging. This wicked chocolate bunny jumped from its place as quickly as the last daylight changed to darkening dusk.

The bunny belonged to Adeline, another boarder in the home. She was thirteen, unrelated, unfriendly and perhaps felt unwanted, too. Emily hesitated but a moment with the Easter bunny in her hand. At first, she only sniffed it. Then she nibbled with a smallest nibble, just the tip of the bunny's left ear. Another nibble to the tip of the right followed, and soon both long ears were gone. By the time Emily replaced the bunny, in the exact same spot, the head had disappeared. There it sat, headless and accusing. When the deed was discovered, Emily lied with large innocent eyes and, for the rest of her life, she knew the taste of shame.

The Brass Rail

Fifty years ago, before women
wore pantsuits, ladies dressed with
white gloves and hats to go shopping.
Mother said, *Ladies never sit at*
a bar. In fact, ladies do not
frequent a bar unescorted.
But there was one time when
Mother broke both these rules.

Two large mahogany carved men were
hanging around the barroom door.
Out of the clear blue, Mother said,
We are going inside for lunch.
This is one bar I want you to see,
she continued as we went from bright
sunlight into near darkness. An aroma
of whiskey floated along with heavy

cigarette smoke from behind
swinging doors of the Brass Rail.
We entered and perched ourselves on
bar stools, unescorted. We ordered
a club sandwich. I was thirteen when
Mother and I broke the rules, when ladies
never did such things. Fifty years later,
I stand on Main Street, Rochester, and

see those same two mahogany men.
Each stands with one foot on a brass rail.
I enter Kruse and Muer Restaurant,
sit at the bar and order a drink.

Anita Elaine Page

Being Eight

I ran outside after the storm
had passed. I was just eight.
I found a fallen sparrow

lying dead and featherless,
surrounded with egg shell
fragments. It was pink and tender.

I picked up the baby bird
and placed it in a red
silk-lined matchbox,

the perfect size
to lay out the fragile babe.
A wake was held and

a burial spot found.
A hole was dug and
comforting words said.

Today, fifty-six years
later, after a storm,
Mother and I are rocking.

She remembers when, just eight,
she found a bird blown
from its nest. She says,

I got a matchbox and
buried the bird . . . and
we are joined in being eight.

Anita Elaine Page

I Remember Christmas Eve

Silence sifts along
like flour spreads
around Mother's baking
at Christmas holiday time.

Sweet smells lift
from high degree ovens
that turn out fresh delights
like sugar plum fairies.

Shared notes sing silent songs
in three corners of my room
as light disappears
into gray shadows.

Half awake, in the fourth corner,
I lie frozen, sleepy-eyed in my bed.
Waiting for midnight strikes,
I listen for the thunder of reindeer hoofs.

Before Artificial Trees

We three children went with Dad
to buy green trees. Going with Father
was an event, an outing after work.
Darkness added adventure.

We were bundled up, with
knitted hats, warm coats, rubber boots.
Frosty breaths froze on loose
scarfs around open necks.

High steps were needed to follow
father's footprints in deep snow
while we heard him barter
for the family Christmas tree.

Dad, a quiet gentle man, had a drink,
or two. Sometimes his courage came
in corked bottles. Listening, we watched.
Prices fell and so did he.

Turning Pages

Grandpa did some funny things
when I was young, like blowing
on newspaper pages to turn them.
I asked, *Why does Grandpa blow
to turn pages? He can't read.*

Mother said, *There are other ways
to learn than reading, and his
fingerprints have worn smooth.
You will see.*

Grandpa could dig a well and
measure materials exactly
in his head. Sometimes he
forgot to shave. I knew
as his beard scratched my face.

But he never forgot to hold
a door for ladies, nor to tip
his hat and rise when they came
into the room. He was soft spoken
though he said his piece.

After a good meal, he would say,
I know I et. Grandpa never
owned a car, or took a plane.
His two-wheeler took him
everywhere he wanted to go.

Now I turn pages with my
smooth prints, and *I know I et.*

Tom

The summer day was golden bright
when Tom and I borrowed
his friend's blue canoe
to paddle across Cass Lake.
We were high school sweethearts
with love as bright as summer sun.

The moment came when young
wisdom let go like a butterfly
first from its cocoon.
I was alone, drifting, floating
smoothly away from shore.

Tom had said, *Wait here,*
but I knew I could paddle
awhile. This soft butterfly
stroked her wings with a slight
paddle. One side, then the other.

Today, Tom is just a speck on shore.
Like a tree, he stands frozen.

Anita Elaine Page

Invisible Thread

Hanging under a blooming catalpa tree,
a little worm climbs an invisible thread.
Wiggling its body, bending in curves,
it becomes a moon crescent
inching its way up a thin line.
Stopping my twilight walk, I wait to watch.

I marvel at this creature's efforts as I watch
it spin and crawl toward the tree's
green leaves. It reminds me of lifelines
shaped by friends, who provided threads
in my life. They were bright crescents
giving hope as I negotiated curves

much too dangerous. Those traveled curves
were beyond wisdom or reason. Yet, a watch
was kept, like a vigil light. A crescent
sliver appears in the evening sky. The tree
shivers in the wind, shaking the thread
and the tiny worm slips backward down the line.

It is easy to cross a fundamental line
of good sense. Just as the worm wiggles and curves
its body, I too, wiggle and curve my core thread.
My tomorrows are present watches
wound in my yesterdays. The catalpa tree
will drop its blossoms and the crescent

will move along my space. There is crescent
light in my thoughts as I write these lines.
Today, I look at the catalpa tree.
Tomorrow, I shall know treacherous curves
around the bend, and I shall keep watch,
struggling in continuation with threads

that weave within my inner core. A thread,
I too, climb an invisible thread. When crescent
moons shine through my window, watching
me settle down to sleep, a long line
of dreams awaken me. Rotating curves
appear in gray shades of bending trees.

I watch them form a horizontal line,
a thread of marching silhouettes. The crescent
moon disappears. I curve. I am the worm.

Mammogram

My right breast,
smooth, firm, tender,
grown from girlhood,
I wanted to hide during
self-conscious puberty.
Full womanhood shows
a body part beautiful,
soft. It desires, nurtures.

Like a death sentence
to be carried out by
an executioner: Biopsy.
Shuddering scenario
that cannot be.
Do not drown me
in this dark sea
of midnight madness!
This is me.
Emotions calm down.

Like a prehistoric giant,
the CAT scan machine
whirls over my body.
It is a metal dinosaur
of another dimension.
It films my innards
without touching me
but breathes a fiery
chill of frosty fingers
that creep through my veins.

Later, a thump sounds.
It happens on the freeway
while driving home.
The rock thrown up
from the darkness outside
matches the blackness inside.

Ragged edges and shattered
headlights are like the surgical
instruments that will
all too soon, slice
and cut at me.
Until I wipe the headlights,
I do not cry: *Mastectomy*.

Anita Elaine Page

The Marlboro Man

He lifts a feather in the wind. Pure and white,
it catches an airy breeze and floats along
light currents, like angel wings whispering
in heavenly skies. A fine delicate finger,
it sails in silence until, out of breath,
it flutters and falls, waiting to be noticed.

Mr. M. passed this way to be noticed.
Seldom were issues black and white.
He spoke his thoughts until his breath
grew its deeper voice. He continued along
his way and lifted no finger
to find answers to questions whispering

inside. His voice grew hoarse and whispered,
Dulce et decorum est, noticed
by Wilfred Owen. It was too late to finger
and beat back the threatening gray white
cloud that hung in the room along
the way. He smoked until each breath

in his lungs exhaled polluted breaths
of puffed nicotine poison, whispering
addiction in his veins. He had to go along
when sirens called, just to be noticed,
to stand out in the crowd. He lifted white
coffin nails, with his brown-stained fingers,

to his mouth and blew out a curling finger
of yellow smoke in each exhaled breath.
The old handkerchief test of white
stained nicotine had no effect with whispering
songs blaring at him, ever begging to be noticed.
Profiteers filled their pockets all along

his shortened life span. He went along
their golden path without lifting a finger
of resistance. Years passed before he noticed
the awful pain of shortness of breath.
He was caught in its grasp. Still whispering,
he gasped, as his cough turned white,

yellow, then red. Soon he noticed each breath
failed to serve him. The smoking gun finger
touched him. He turned stone cold white.

A Still Day

It's a still day. It's a still day.
Leaves hang like artificial
replicas of themselves. Shiny, waxy dust
laden greens of various hues reflect
sounds stirring in the dawn.
A roar enters the conversation.

Move to Continuing Care, she says in conversational
tones. It shouts at all defences. The day
she brought you home in her arms, a dawn
of pain-mixed joy replaced all artificial
thoughts from her. Mellow, she reflects
as to escape the bitter dust.

Turning from you, she turns to dust
the tabletops marred with remnant conversation.
Scars from blocks and toy cars reflect
the sweetness of tiny hands from another day.
Shocking screeches tear loose artificial
words that linger on her lips at dawn.

Yes, she says, *no use being a burden. It dawns
on me, the time to go is near.* She dusts
the rocker in which she rocked you. No artificial
word can replace the wonder years of conversation
at her knee. *You are grown so tall. A day
will come when you will be like me, reflect*

this moment over the years. A time to reflect
comes to everyone. Memories filter like the dawn
as you recall paths taken. As a still day
settles the landscape, dreams and passions will rise like dust
Sounds will flow, like this conversation,
back and forth until a decision is made. Artificial

hopes fade into nothingness, suppressed by artificial
toys to fill the void. With scores of years, reflection
comes in radiant light toward a peak conversation.
Continuing Care, she says. *Yes, yes, in the dawn
drawing near I will go. For I know, soon it is dust
I will be*. Looking out the window on a still day,

you will hold your conversation and see the waxy green dawn.
When the roar has settled, an artificial replica will reflect
the swirling dust at your feet on a still day.

Anita Elaine Page

I Weep Inside

Today, the death of the red oak, radiant
in front of our window, causes me to grieve.
This sturdy old tree has graced our landscape for years
and shielded life through ravages of storm
and blight. I weep inside as it is felled
and ground to wood chips in such few hours.

Now, through a shuttered window, I see hours
unblocked by shades of green that grow radiant
in the sunlight. I think of buildings and trees felled
by shells exploding in Bosnia-Herzegovina; I grieve
for refugees, for children caught in an age-old storm
that ravages their land in hatreds from past years.

The oak stump, with age-rings stilled, shows years
of growth in peace and harmony, but long hours
are present in the eye of the storm.
Raw earth bleeds sawdust, catches radiant
sunbeams shifting in the wind to better grieve
the plight of those who march over those who fell.

The root system's brief breaths remain beneath its felled
tree trunk. Breathing, gasping, it holds years
now gone. Looking at the destruction makes me grieve
for the red oak that yesterday, today, just hours
before, stood guarding, shielding, sharing radiant
life in its glory. The blight spreads like a tropical storm.

It rages and grows to hurricane force, a storm
that must be reckoned with before everything is felled
in its path. The powers-that-be stand in radiant
powerlessness. History does repeat itself through the years.
It comes to haunt humanity in its darkest hours.
I grieve for the tree, the people. For you and me, I grieve.

Families are torn, men slaughtered, women raped and I grieve.
I grieve for violators caught in the monstrous storm
that destroys their souls. When night comes and dawn hours
wake, how do they survive the silence of their souls felled
in their own destruction? Children's faces shall haunt for years
and years. Orphan cries shall rise to radiant

echo of funeral marches, and no amount of hours
sung shall take their memories away. The world shall grieve
their strife and plant more trees for years and years and years.

Dreams of Gold

Sunlight filters behind gathering clouds,
while December's first cold freezes deeper pond waters.
Little critters and birds sleep in nests
out of sight. Beneath this frosty breath,

my soul shivers. Inside, I wrap packages
with reds, greens, golds, ribbon shades,
bright bows and paper. I remember dreams
that sleep amid holiday bustle
of lights and tinsel. Fresh pine boughs are

warm and dry. They prick and fall.
No comfort, no thought is given to creatures
that wander and breathe in empty forests, or vacant lots.
I insulate myself and pull the shade
of indifference, before I cry.

Optimistic dreams of my youth are silent voices now.
They are asleep, not gone. Dormant,
they wait to find renewal in the young
who will come to challenge and raise the shades
drawn by earlier generations.

Fresh hopes in shades of red, yellow, black and
white will find comfort in humanity.
Created equal will breathe
a new equality of purpose. Democracy,
ever fresh, will inflame the human spirit.

Pure waters eternally flow toward a new age.
Neighbors will purify themselves in celebration
of opening shades for children everywhere.
Tuning sleeping hearts with hope renewed,
peace flows, and we stand in golden shade.

Equilibrium

I reveal myself in reverie,
wish back some twenty years
to quieter times and silent sounds,
while I sit on the deck.

Present in the chatter and songs of birds,
winds push layers of green and
rush past wings that move
above the roar of cement trucks
and constant traffic hums.

High, sometimes low, they rumble
and assault my inner solstice.
In nature's harmony
an equilibrium
returns to the soul.

Winds of Conscience

Willow trees bend in horizontal lean
with gray winds sweeping forgotten leaves.
Raindrops whip to icy needles that cling
in autumn's end. Blowing snow flurries howl
and whistle wispy tunes of haunting sounds.

November settles. Squirrel chatter, bird songs
are strangely quiet, sleep to earth's time.
Cold foreboding days tell the changing season
to blow as far as winds can go.
I hear a voice that speaks to my deceit.

Autumn's sleep turns restless in echos
of lost innocence. I cannot lean on anyone,
for I am grown old and have nowhere
to hide inside. What sounds are these
I hear? Hate sighs, like ovens burning flesh.

Not so? But, I hold to regrets. Tell me,
how to leave it go, how to sing
a new heart song of love and joy,
and let go old ways that climb pillars of rage.
Who to blame? Blowing winds stir me.

Still, I keep my old ways. When will I learn
new notes? I know, I must sing them before
I leave this place. I listen to the autumn wind
to know myself and move toward the light.
Songs are different when conscience leans.

Seashell

Smooth, empty clustered shell,
fossils washed in stormy seas
are chipped, broken, bonded
like a sunset upon the shore.

Ocean waves twirl, toss and
float tiny clinging creatures.
Colonies huddle in lost
clusters of family life.

Linda C. Angér
A Simple Shift in Cadence

I Write My Name

With curly serifs of praise and celebration
On paper, wood, snapshots, or cement
With spears of anger and fear
In precise script or loopy strokes
With the hue of my eyes and thoughts
On matchbooks, keychains, or
Christmas stockings
With the song of my words and actions
In pastel crayons or neon inks
With my dance of desire against convention
On trees, where it will last forever

I write my name in hopes someone will
recognize it—
and take me home for good.

Linda C. Angér

Dancer

I always wanted to be a dancer,

to step boldly in rhythms
of awareness, like a wraith,
to move lithely in both form and essence,
absorbed and changed
by a simple shift in cadence,
unfaltering in syncopated time,

to master the sultry samba
of lips on the verge of a kiss,
to sway with the waltz of hand-to-breast,
to immortalize in movement
the holiness of a single embrace,
transformed in the accent of a sigh,

to dip wide-eyed, allegro,
between hope and fear,
to welcome the adagio of solitude, dancing,
where even stillness becomes motion.

Linda C. Angér

Between the Leaves

Don't rake these fallen gold and russet leaves,
let them decompose in autumn rains,
in sleepy garden beds, with memories
you've gathered up since spring.

The time has come for me to leave,
while yellow mums still grace our cobbled path,
before the frigid glance, the frost-cloaked words.
I've never weathered out a rugged winter.

It's April air I love, fresh-scented, sweet
and cool, as we were those first days.
Buds grow to wide-leafed oaks and maples;
handshakes turn to passionate embrace.

We grew love like forget-me-nots,
believing hardy roots hold ever-strong.
Then came the summer solstice of our hearts:
warm air turned chill, sweet petals lost their scent.

Don't rake your fallen gold and russet dreams,
but let them decompose in autumn rains
or fallow garden beds, rich food
for love's be-leafing your next spring.

Linda C. Angér

Reading Rumi

The Sufi says:
When two unite in love, or hate,
a spirit third is born.
These Beings live within the ethers,
have form, speech and vision.
They must be gently tended.

While scents of your body still
linger on my skin,
and voices of your seed still
echo in my womb,
you ask me to no longer breath you in, or listen.

Who will tend the spirit children we gave life?
They are fervent words, impassioned kisses,
churning in my belly.
Mirrors of loving and discord,
they do not know you've gone.

Wraith-like and hungry, they wail behind
my swollen eyes;
I strain to lay their shadows down,
but reach them only when I breath, or listen.

Night Visit

I wake at night,
feel you curled against my spine.
I wrap myself in you.

I wake, aware it was not
a dream, but still,
it is a mystery.

I touch the place I thought you'd been.
Perhaps are. Again
I sleep, content.

○

Duality

Your demanding voice
on the phone
slices through me
like a rusty blade.

My belly thuds
like a stone
on damp earth,
unable to howl
leave me alone,

while you hear
only my soft
hello.

Linda C. Angér

Wallpapering

Measuring our time like lengths of paper,
you fit our interactions to your social plumb line,
insist on perfect seams. You tell me:
A good wallpaper hides a thousand sins.

But I would rather feel the bumps
and indentations of bare plaster
than be tricked by the
symmetry of patterned facades.

I won't stick it out —

you'd want to brush me flat,
a muted rose on your traditional wall.
I'd dance barefoot
up a makeshift ladder, crying:
Hand me the steamer, Honey,
this paper's coming down.

Linda C. Angér

Mama's Closet

Mama hid everything in her walk-in closet, like the bag of marijuana and string bikini she found in my sister Nancy's purse. Of course, Nancy knew where to look; Mama never threw anything away. Her closet was stuffed with old lace dresses and feathered hats. Teddy bears and Christmas aprons crouched among shoes she had not worn in 20 years. Glass jars full of buttons from worn-out clothes blinked between papered hat-boxes.

I would sit on the deep shelf behind pastel crinolines, reading the stack of yellowed letters from somewhere in the South Pacific, or try to play Dad's bass drum with my tiny bare hands.

The scents and textures of past and present mingled there: a museum, a holding place for the unresolved difficulties of marriage and parenthood. As a child, I wondered why she saved all those useless things, why she put the things she took from our rooms in the one place she knew we would look. Perhaps it was the only way she could declare her knowledge of our doings without imposing her control.

Last week, I found a *Playboy* magazine under my son's mattress. I left it there. My closet is full enough, with bags of bell-bottom jeans, go-go boots, and a stack of yellowed letters from somewhere in Southeast Asia.

Bone Surgery

Men in white coats
thunder down the hall.
I hear their stern voices oozing
words too big to fit their stringent lips,
like records played too slow.
I rupture from my child body, tense
and pale, on a cold steel table.
Their clammy hands probe and twist my limbs.

Men in white coats
never look at my face;
they call me *specimen*,
gash cold silver toys through my skin, stab
needles in my howling veins,
carve my bones like roasted
fowl, command me to stop crying.

I fracture, flee to soft gray mist
where no acid voices rasp,
no fleshy hands slap
trembling mouths.
In mist, I am
not shamed or broken.

Linda C. Angér

Inheritance

In this old house nothing is ever lost.
The murmers of long-ago love-talk,
the brown aroma of beef-barley soup,
the strains of a plaintive violin—
all cling to flocked wallpaper.

Secrets are dust on a shuttered window pane,
bootlegged whiskey in the cellar,
stolen chocolate from the five-and-dime,
a mistress on the other side of town.

Unfinished arguments, blue ribbons,
childhood sweethearts, black eyes
awake to slip from furniture and walls at night;
they are contented sighs and soulful tremors.

Lives layer, passing eyes
and chins through generations,
china cups through tiers of grandmas;
bridal veils are tucked in scented tissue.

In this old house nothing ever dies.
Shadows live in vaulted ceilings,
soak up the passing days,
and hold the walls together.

A Recipe for Hysteria

Lock all your emotion in a safe-deposit box. Tabulate the good-to-bad news ratio in the morning paper. Do ten sit-ups, eat a chocolate donut as reward. Stand on the bathroom scale and gasp. Don't smile, don't touch, don't laugh, don't look anyone in the eye. Read election campaign literature and convince yourself the candidates are sane. Calculate your net worth. Judge yourself against an unreachable scale of perfection. Blame everyone you know for all that's wrong in your life. Consider the worst-case scenario and know that it will happen to you. Make assumptions about everyone you meet, and what they are thinking about you. Set your alarm clock for right now, push the "constant repeat" button.

Recipe for Inner Peace

Pour equal parts truth, clarity and willingness into your left ear. Jump up and down twenty-one times, then sit quietly until you feel bubbling light all around you. Tilt your right ear into the sink, watch slammed doors, chewed fingernails, racist jokes, third helpings, and tear-stained pillows go down the drain. Rinse thoroughly with clear intention. See yourself and everyone else complete and innocent. Prepare a large meal of nourishing words, tender touch, juicy hugs and kisses; garnish with kind smiles and honest eyes. Share it with everyone you meet. Eat until big belly laughs roll out of you, and notice the plate is never empty.

Linda C. Angér

Heroin

All the kisses mama withheld,
you say,
while your hollow eyes
search
for spoons and matches.

Better than any lover,
you say,
while your fumbling hands
prepare
another needle.

I'll check into rehab tomorrow morning,
you say,
while your veins bulge
under rubber tubing.

I know I'll stay clean this time,
you say,
but I'd die for one last fix tonight.

And you do,
a needleful of kisses
piercing the
whiteness of your
inner thigh,
where a lover
might have dreamt.

Linda C. Angér

Increments

My little boy, who'd tumble in my arms on
stormy nights, share details of his day over spaghetti
and apple pie, has disappeared,
replaced in increments
by a phantom
who leaves me notes in a strong, masculine hand:
I need ten bucks, or
Please buy more shaving cream.
He programs mysterious one-touch phone numbers,
wears dress shirts and Italian leather jackets.

I hear him slip out late at night,
see his tire tracks in my snowy driveway.
But his hands and face and voice
no longer join me for the evening news
or Sunday dinner.

Now I hear only the creaking of the walls,
the second-hand tick from the mantle clock,
so slow it must be broken.

Linda C. Angér

My Man Can Be So Irritating

I don't mean the wayward socks and shirts
that never make it to the hamper,

or bitter words that scorch my heart,
forgotten anniversaries, or unmowed lawns.

I have no profound insight on gender differences,
or the politics of why God is called *He* instead of *It*.

I'm referring to that numb redness
of my skin after we make love,

how his evening stubble rakes across my body,
leaving tiny rivers that fill with pain and pleasure

and tingle there for days.

Linda C. Angér

Stole and Tails

Refused entry at the door,
we laughed our way home
in soggy jeans and
laceless sneakers,
down puddled April streets.

You, stuffed in a moth-holed
cutaway with fraying tails,
me, mummied up in some dead
flapper's fringed silk stole,
$2.50 each at the Salvation Army.

A strain to our budget, but
the invitation read:
Formal attire required.

Linda C. Angér

The Waiter

The waiter, young and confident,
presents a flawless meal.
His white shirt crackles;
manicured fingers place saucer
and goblet with precision.

But still, I am a better waiter.
After all, I have been waiting all my life—
for a better time, a better idea,
a better job, a better lover.

His hair is rich, distinctly styled.
My hair grows wild and gray.
I linger over coffee; he glances again at his watch.
I calculate my evening, leave a proper tip.

He shuts the lights behind me; we walk in opposite directions.
We've both had enough of waiting.

Linda C. Angér

Menopause

Perhaps I fear my days grow shorter
as the moon deserts my womb,
or that my womanness will
bleed away, in dried-out joints
and fractured memory.

This decades-old regularity,
a rythmic hinge on which
I plan weekends with a lover,
safe times to wear white trousers,
now comes erratically,
a discordant trickle that shifts
the contours of my breasts and spine,
shifts the cadence of my life.

No longer virile-wombed, not yet a barren crone
but adrift between these worlds,
I've fallen out of tune with lunar cycles,
and hear my dead grandmothers
begin to call me home.

Linda C. Angér

The Afterlife of Roses

Hannah brought flowers to every birth and death in the neighborhood. Her bouquet was always the same— a single red rose, a white carnation, and a sprig of ladyfern tied with a black satin ribbon.

The other children were afraid of her, the odd old woman at the end of the street. But I had seen enough of Hannah mending broken wings and growing lush garden beds, in soil farmers had forsaken, to trust the gentle wisdom beneath her ancient, stern appearance. I alone would meet her eye through the foliage as I hop-scotched down the sidewalk with the other girls. I alone would journey into her yard and eventually her home, to learn things long forgotten yet still alive, things made of mystery yet more real than the earth under our feet.

When I was five, my cat tangled with a speeding car and lost. Hannah slipped through the hedge between our land and hers, to stand at dusk above the grave my father had dug for Buttercup's broken body. She spoke softly, then moved back through the hedge, without bending a branch. I could not see clearly in the dim light, but I knew she had left something there. Weaving my way through the yard, pretending nonchalance, I came upon the grave only after fawning over flowerbeds, playing on the old rope-and-tire swing, and finally arriving as if totally surprised to find myself there. She'd left a small bouquet— one perfect miniature red rose, one white dwarf carnation, and one single sprig of ladyfern, tied with a black satin ribbon.

Her piercing, gentle gray eyes caught mine through the dark hedge, now flecked with fading daylight. Nothing moved as she spoke. "Release life back to itself, little one. Let go of your tears and your pet. Release him, release yourself." I untied the satin knot. The flowers sprawled across the mound of dirt. Hannah drew a sharp, deep breath. "It is done," she whispered through the branches. My sorrow was gone. Hannah vanished from beyond the hedge.

From my room that night, I watched shadows dance in the flicker of candlelight through the curtains of her windows. My dreams were filled with strange, exotic plants and aromas. I walked old forest paths, woven-handed with Hannah. When morning came, I moved through the hedge without bending a branch.

Over the years, Hannah taught me everything she knew of gardening; we spent hours planting and mulching, pruning and aerating. Her yard was a maze of plots and pots. In time, I came to know the secret names and uses for hundreds of flowers and herbs. Hannah taught me to carefully slice all but one woody thorn from a rose stem, to steep petals and leaves for teas and medicines. I learned to gauge the passage of the season in the gentle unfolding of a rosebud, to welcome bees and earthworms as much as birds and butterflies. It became my job to keep her informed of expectant mothers and impending deaths in our neighborhood. Together we would hunt out the perfect blossoms, tending them for days in anticipation of their carefully prepared function. Together we would label and store the ointments, salves and tinctures she used to heal aching joints or broken hearts throughout the winter months, while the gardens rested under deep snow.

The ritual for a birthing was different than for a death, although the ingredients were the same. Hannah would arrive at a birthing with the pieces of her gift stored in separate pockets. She assembled the bouquet as she stood over the cradle, speaking so only the child could hear, and left immediately after her gifting was complete. The satin knots were left intact.

And so I passed from childhood to womanhood, tending gardens and neighbors with Hannah. Marriage and a house two-hundred miles away made my trips home sporadic and far too short; ten years passed before I went to visit for the summer.

Hannah and her gardens had grown sparse and dry. The vibrant dahlias of my youth were gone, the coreopsis beds taken over by weeds and wild grasses. Scarlet roses, dying on the stem, turned the color of old dried blood. White carnations were almost transparent, like the rice-paper skin stretched over her hands.

In her old bentwood rocker, which I'd move outside each morning, Hannah would watch as I cleared overgrown beds, planted healthy seeds and began to gather flowers. Within weeks, her gardens had returned to their earlier splendor. Hannah was the most radiant I had seen her in decades, despite her increased frailty.

I laughed when she gave me the hickory-twig broom her teacher had made a century ago. I wept when she forced me to pack the journals of her recipes and procedures, begun when she was 13, into a box for shipment to my home. Hannah died at midsummer, in her 95th year. I waited at the funeral home, but no one came. The street belonged to strangers now. My childhood friends and neighbors had long since moved away, or died themselves.

And when the minister had read his psalms and epistles, when the funeral director stood ready to extinguish the candles, I placed my bouquet over her heart— a single red rose, a white carnation, and a sprig of ladyfern, tied with a black satin ribbon. I spoke so only she could hear; I spoke the words she'd taught me years ago:

Red for the blood of woman,
white for the seed of man,
green for the earth you walked upon,
and black for the mystery that binds them

I untied the satin knot. The flowers sprawled across her breast, and I heard Hannah whisper, "It is done." My sorrow was gone.

My daughter, Hannah, was born the next spring. Last night, just five-years-old, she moved through the hedge without bending a branch.

David Sabbagh
Pilot to Control Tower

I sit at the controls.
I've been circling too long,
and I need to land.
Surrounded by choices,
I decide to try a few.

                  i m b .
               l
            c

Pushing this button, I
Pulling that lever, I

            d
              i
                v e .

Suddenly,
I realize,
I don't know what I'm doing.
Looking around for any kind of assistance,
I open a manual only to read:

       This page intentionally left blank.

Frantically, I radio for help.
Pilot to control tower, I shout. *I need some instruction.*
Static is all I hear.

Entry Visa

The Director of Immigration and Naturalization was still deep in his thoughts on what he should say to the President and his staff when the door to the inner office opened and the meeting coordinator appeared.

"The President and his Cabinet are ready to see you," spoke the coordinator in a hushed tone.

"Thank you," said the Director as he stood and walked towards the Coordinator.

"Mr. President," said the Coordinator, "the Director of Immigration, Mr. Whitehead, is next on the agenda."

"Thank you, Cathy," said the President. "So, Mr. Whitehead, what business do you bring us?"

"Well, Mr. President, I have an application for a visa from a very important person, and I feel I shouldn't be the one to decide whether or not to allow this person entry into the United States."

"Who is it, some political dissident or exiled dictator?"

"Actually, sir, it's. . . Jesus."

"Oh, then it *is* some exiled Latin American dictator."

"No, sir, Jesus. You know, the Bible, Christmas?" said Mr. Whitehead meekly.

"What?!?" shouted the President. "My Cabinet and I have important issues to cover today, and we don't have time for joking around!"

"I . . . I know what you must be thinking," stammered the Director, "I thought exactly the same thing when two of my subordinates brought me the application but, after you hear me out on this, I think you'll believe it, too."

"Okay, answer me this. Why would Jesus choose the United States to visit, and why would he bother to apply for an entry visa?"

"I'm afraid I don't have concrete answers for you," said the Director. "They always say that the Lord works in mysterious ways. And, there has been a lot of boasting by several groups that the United States is a Christian country. Maybe this is some kind of a test to see if that's true?"

"I suppose that's possible," said the President, "but just what makes you so sure that application is from Jesus?"

"It's strange, sir, but when I have the application in my hands, a powerful feeling comes over me that makes me believe it's authentic. And, the two subordinates who brought me the application said the same thing happened to them."

"Okay, give it to me and let's see what happens."

The Director's nervousness intensified as he noticed that all the members of the President's Cabinet were glaring at him, no doubt waiting to reassign him to some US Governmental office in Siberia should his claim be proven false. Finally, in what seemed to be an excruciatingly long period of time, the President looked at his Director of Immigration and said, "Well, approve his visa."

"I'll carry out your order immediately," said the Director, reaching for the application.

Mr. Whitehead was about to take the application from the President when, suddenly, the Chief of Staff said, "I think we had better talk about this some more, Mr. President."

The Director stopped immediately, and a slightly audible gasp emanated from several of the room's inhabitants. "Why should there be any question about giving Jesus our approval to enter this country?" said the President, retracting the application. "Do you realize what a visit from Jesus will do to my approval rating? When the public sees that Jesus wants to have a meeting with me, it'll skyrocket!"

"Maybe so, but don't you think that Jesus' arrival is going to be pretty disruptive?" said the Chief of Staff.

"I don't think it's anything we can't handle, if we are given enough time to prepare," said the President.

"I'm not talking about crowd control or what hotel Jesus should stay in when he gets here. I'm talking about a fundamental disruption to our society."

"Okay, so go on."

"If I remember my Sunday school lessons correctly," said the Chief of Staff, "aren't there going to be a thousand years of peace when Jesus comes back from Heaven?"

"Yeah, that's correct."

"So, two weeks ago we gave the Pentagon an extra 7 billion

dollars for next year. We barely got the increase past the public, even though the Cold War is over, but nobody will accept even a dime going for defense because there will be no more wars."

"In fact," whined the Secretary of Defense, "who's even going to think we need the armed forces. . . or, even a Secretary of Defense!?"

"In that case, we certainly won't need a defense industry," sputtered the Secretary of Labor.

"Yes," said the President, "that could be pretty disruptive, but I still think this will be a great opportunity for us. Hell, we'll finally get the chance to settle a few of the social debates that are going on in this country."

"Yes, that's true, Mr. President," argued the Chief of Staff, "but there are other reasons we might want to reconsider allowing Jesus to enter our country. For example, Jesus has never been fond of money lenders. What do you think he would say about our business establishment? Do you realize how many billions are made just by the credit card industry alone?"

"You're right, they are some of our party's bigger contributors. Anybody else have arguments to make?"

"Um, I do, Mr. President," said the Secretary of Commerce.

"Well, what's your argument?"

"You know, Jesus never did amass any kind of fortune during his life. In fact, he probably didn't own anything except the clothes he wore."

"Annnnnd . . . ." prompted the President.

"And, if people suddenly decide to live a simple life like he did, what's going to happen to the rest of our economy?"

"Hmmm, I hadn't thought of that," muttered the President. "Frank, you haven't said anything. Do you have any concerns?"

"As a matter of fact," said the Secretary of Housing and Urban Development, "Jesus is not going to be pleased by the plight of the poor children in our country."

"I'm beginning to think this application is not the blessing I originally thought it would be," said the President. "Are there any final arguments?"

"Well, yes," said the Chief of Staff, "and it deals directly with us. Do you remember 'The Sermon on the Mount' where Jesus said that 'the meek shall inherit the earth?' "

"I remember," said the President.

"So, what do you think that means to us? Could any of us be considered meek? Could any elected official be considered meek or powerless? Not likely. And, if Jesus is true to his word, we aren't going to be in power much longer, either. No, Mr. President, I don't think we should approve Jesus' visa application."

"I can't argue with that but, if we deny the visa, do you think Jesus will even abide by our decision? He might enter this country anyway!"

"Well, Mr. President, he accepted the officials' judgments during his lifetime, so I imagine he will this time."

"I hope you're right. Mr. Whitehead," said the President, handing the application back to the Director of Immigration. "Prepare and sign a letter stating that, at this particular time, we cannot approve Jesus' application for an entry visa."

O

The lifegiving drop of water
falls to the ground,
only to evaporate.

The Favor

"Matthew, come here for a minute. I want you to do a favor for me," yelled Matthew's mother, making sure she could be heard from her place in the kitchen.

Matthew sat there pretending he hadn't heard his mother. It wasn't that he didn't want to do favors for her. It was just that she always seemed to ask for them while he was watching his favorite TV shows.

"Matthew, get in here this minute," his mother yelled impatiently.

"What is it Mom?" asked Matthew as he entered the kitchen.

"Matthew, I want you to get me two bottles of pop from the basement."

Of all the favors he was asked to do, going to the basement alone was the absolute worst. To a seven-year-old boy, the basement meant only one thing— monsters. "Anybody who watches the 'Saturday Night Monster Movies,'" thought Matthew, "knows there are trolls hiding under the basement stairs, psycho killers lurking behind the furnace, and child-eating lizard-people living in the big water-filled hole that leads to the center of the earth."

"Are you sure there isn't any pop up here?" said Matthew, hoping that somehow his mother had experienced a sudden lapse in memory.

"Yes, I'm sure," said his mother tiredly.

"I *know* we don't have any more pop downstairs," said Matthew, hoping to convince his mother not to send him to the monster pit.

"Matthew, we have pop because your father brought some home yesterday."

"Why can't Billy go downstairs and get the pop? He never has to do anything," Matthew whined, making one last effort to escape becoming lizard food, or possibly a troll slave, by offering his little brother to the monsters.

"Matthew, your brother is too young. Now get down there and bring up some pop!" his mother said, pausing after each word.

Matthew saw that his mother was becoming angry with him and realized that he was on the verge of receiving one or more of her dastardly punishments if he didn't go down into the basement. Matthew paused for a moment, trying to decide which fate would be worse— no T.V. or being eaten. Since he had never really seen any monsters before but he had experienced several groundings, Matthew decided to take his chances with the monsters.

Descending the stairs, Matthew was deep in thought about how he could safely reach the light switch that was next to the refrigerator. His heart began to race the instant he stepped off the landing into the eerie darkness. As he ventured further into the basement, the hairs on his neck stood up and he felt sure the monsters could hear the beating of his heart. Walking as quietly as possible lest he signal the monsters that their dinner had arrived, his destination seemed a thousand miles away. "Why couldn't Mom get the pop?" he thought. "Monsters never eat grown-ups."

About halfway to the refrigerator, Matthew heard a whirring and slurping noise coming from the big hole in the floor. His dad once told him the noise came from an elevator bringing the child-eating lizard people up from the center of the earth. He also said if Matthew ever heard that kind of a noise, he should run without looking back. Otherwise, the lizard people might catch him and make a meal out of him. Matthew's heart jumped into his throat as he took off in terror for the staircase. He reached the stairs safely, but it didn't matter. His journey wasn't over. He knew he couldn't go back to the kitchen empty-handed because his Mom would not only punish him, she would still make him go back downstairs and get the pop. Matthew had to think up another plan.

"This time," he thought, "I'll run to the refrigerator, grab the pop and get out before the monsters have a chance to figure out what's going on."

"Three, two, one," counted Matthew in a feeble attempt to give himself confidence before starting his dash to the basement light. He took off for the refrigerator and, upon reaching it, began jumping and flailing wildly until he was able to grab the string to the light fixture and pull it. Matthew grabbed the bottles in his arms and was closing the refrigerator door, when suddenly the same whirring and slurping noise started again. In an instant, the hair on Matthew's neck stood at attention and his eyes widened in panic. Not wanting to see the lizard people, Matthew took off for the staircase, pop bottles in hand. Knowing the lizard people were on to him, and it would only be seconds before they notified the trolls and the psycho killer, Matthew bounded up the basement steps two at a time and lunged into the kitchen.

"Here's the pop you wanted," said Matthew in a tone that hid the sheer magnitude of the risk he had just taken for his mother.

"Thank you, Matthew. You're such a good boy. Oh, and Matthew, did you remember to turn out the lights?"

Somewhere in the Middle

"Hey guy, what's goin' on," said Steve enthusiastically as he sat down with Jerry.

"Ahhh, not much," sighed Jerry.

"Woah, man, you sound bummed. What happened?"

"Joyce dumped me last week."

"What!?" said Steve in disbelief. "Two weeks ago you guys were joined at the hip."

"I know," said Jerry evenly. "I'm still kinda stunned. I really thought we had potential because we had so much in common: working out, reading, cooking, outdoor activities — everything seemed to say we were going to be an item."

"Yeah, you two did seem pretty compatible," said Steve.

"I thought I was doing everything right. I called when I said I would, I showed up at her apartment on time, I was attentive, I sent her flowers, I even wrote her a nice poem. I thought women *liked* being treated that way," Jerry said as the tone of his voice raised, revealing his exasperation.

"I know what you're saying," said Steve. "You hear women complaining up and down about how men are dogs, but when they meet one that treats them nicely, they say he's too boring."

"Man, this sucks," said Jerry. "Does this mean I have to learn to be a jerk just to get anywhere with women?"

"Come on, just be like you've always been. If they don't like it, then the hell with them," said Steve.

"Yeah, I suppose you're right."

"Do you think Joyce was dating somebody else when you met her?"

"Nah, I doubt it. I don't see how she could since we spent so much time together," said Jerry.

"So, when did you notice a change in her attitude?"

"After our date last week."

"What'd you do to her?"

"Nothing," said Jerry, his voice raising in pitch again, "the whole day was perfect, except maybe for dinner. Even though Joyce said she liked it, I was still a little embarrassed."

"Why? You're a great cook."

"Thanks. The problem was that I told her I was going to make some spaghetti sauce from scratch. Unfortunately, I worked a ton of hours that week and couldn't get to the grocery store, so I didn't have squat in my fridge. I ended up making the spaghetti using some ready-made sauce."

"Did you tell her about the sauce?" said Steve.

"No. I really didn't think she would notice the sauce was store—bought."

"So far, it doesn't sound like you did anything that would make her not want to see you anymore," said Steve. "You must have done something else."

"I don't know. After dinner I was feeling romantic . . . ."

"You mean horny," interrupted Steve.

"Yeah, whatever. Anyway, I began to put some moves on her and one thing led to another and we ended up in my bedroom."

"That explains it. Maybe I should introduce myself to her so she can meet a real man," said Steve sarcastically.

"Gee, thanks pal. Plunge the knife in a little deeper, why don't you?" said Jerry,

"Sorry, just trying to cheer you up."

"Ahh, that's all right. I'm still a little pissed off. Besides, that was the point when things seemed to go downhill."

"What do you mean?"

"Well, I wanted to make her laugh by pretending I was this macho jerk. I figured she'd catch the sarcasm because I hardly have any muscles, and she knows I don't act like a macho jerk."

"So what did you do?"

"I jokingly told her to get in bed and strip. Then I came swaggering out of the bathroom flexing my muscles and wearing that pair of gag underwear I won at Kevin's bachelor party last year."

"Please say you really didn't do that," said Steve. "When are you going to learn that it takes more than just a few weeks for somebody to understand your sense of humor?"

"I know, I know," sighed Jerry. "Joyce must have thought I was a complete jerk."

"At least I hope the sex was good," said Steve.

"I thought it was great, although I was so tired from working all those hours. I fell asleep almost immediately afterwards. I really felt bad, but I just couldn't help it."

"Do you think Joyce will give you another chance?"

"No way. She got pissed off about something and wanted me to take her home that night. When I dropped her off at her apartment, she said we couldn't go out any more."

"Bummer," said Steve.

"Yeah, I know," sighed Jerry. "So do you want to go out this Friday night?"

○

"I can't believe I fell for another jerk," said Joyce, staring at the bottom of the empty cup she was holding.

"What are you talking about?" said Jan.

"I mean, I was fooled by yet another guy."

"Who was it this time?"

"Jerry."

"You mean the guy you met at the Watering Hole? The one you said could be Mr. Right?" exclaimed Jan in a tone of disbelief.

"Yeah, that's the one. The man who said all the things I wanted to hear. God, I feel like such a fool."

"Come on, don't be so hard on yourself. Men can be pretty good liars when they want to be."

"I know, but I thought Jerry was going to be different."

"Oh yeah, what happened?" asked Jan.

"Well, the first two weeks were really nice. He called me when he said he would, he was prompt, he took me to nice restaurants, he sent me flowers, he even wrote me a poem. I couldn't believe he was for real, because most guys aren't so attentive."

"Yeah, I've seen some like that. They're great until you sleep with them but, the second it's finished, they turn into creeps," said Jan.

"Isn't that the truth. Anyway, last week Jerry said he wanted to take me on a super-romantic date, so we spent the day at a nice park. Then he cooked dinner for me back at his apartment. The first part of the date at the park was nice. It was when we got back to his place that things went downhill."

"He didn't want to sit down and watch sports, did he?" asked Jan.

"No, it wasn't that."

"So, what did he do wrong?"

"It's not that he did anything wrong. It's just that I started noticing some inconsistencies between what he'd told me on previous dates and what I saw in his apartment."

"Yeah, like what?"

"Well, he mentioned several times how much he was into working out and also how he liked to cook healthy meals but, when I went into his refrigerator to get something to drink, I didn't see any food that a health-nut would eat. He only had some beer, a few carrots, and a piece of cheesecake."

"I guess that would make me wonder," said Jan. "But there must have been something worse to make you this disgusted with him."

"Don't worry, the story gets better. Jerry also said he made the spaghetti using an old recipe of his Italian grandmother's but, when I was getting my drink, I noticed an almost empty jar of spaghetti sauce hidden in the back of the fridge."

"It amazes me," said Jan, "that men think we're so stupid we'll completely fall for anything they tell us."

"Yeah, I know," said Joyce. "Seeing that empty jar made me start wondering about everything else he's told me since we've been together. It just didn't make sense, though, that a guy who would write a poem for me would lie about dinner."

"He probably copied the poem from somewhere," said Jan.

"Oh, I don't know. The poem wasn't that good."

"Did you ask to go home?"

"No, my heart wanted me to believe that he really was a nice guy, so I decided to see how the rest of the evening turned out."

"Well, what happened?"

"Ummmm."

"You slept with him, didn't you?" exclaimed Jan.

"Yesssss. I guess I just had a little too much wine."

"So, was he any good?"

"He was good if you like being bossed around, having quick sex, and being ignored. I mean, can you believe he ordered me to lie on his bed and take my clothes off while he was in the bathroom getting ready?"

"Jeez, what an unromantic slug," said Jan.

"You think that's bad. He came swaggering out of his bathroom posing like one of those bodybuilders. Only he hardly had any muscles to show off. The funniest thing though, was that he wore these bikini briefs with 'Home of the Whopper' printed on the front of them. I should have sued him for false advertising," said Joyce trying to contain her laughter. "Anyway, we started and the next thing I knew we, or I should say he, finished. After that, he rolled over and went to sleep. That was the last straw; I woke Jerry up and asked him to take me home."

"How did he take it?" said Jan.

"He seemed surprised that I would want to leave. I guess he just didn't get it. In fact, even after I hardly spoke to him during the car ride, he still didn't get the message and asked me out again!"

"Please don't say you accepted," pleaded Jan.

"No way! I told him we couldn't go out anymore."

"Good for you," said Jan. "You did the right thing telling him to take a hike."

"Thanks. So, do you want to go out this Friday night?"

O

An empty vessel sits,
containing only darkness.
Goodbye was spoken.

David Sabbagh

Hooray, It's Christmas

To whom it may concern:

I, Santa Claus, am suffering from career burnout and will soon be resigning as chief executive officer of North Pole Industries. The rewards I get from Christmas are overshadowed by new aggravations, and I don't have the stamina to make it through many more holiday seasons.

The source of my frustration is not so much the Christmas holiday, it's the preparation for Christmas Eve. Two hundred years ago, I started the preparations in October. At that time, I would make sure the elves were underway building toys and then, sometime after Thanksgiving, I would begin preparing for the big flight. Because of the complications brought about by modern technology, though, I've had to put in much longer days. Now, the elves are working split shifts year round, and I begin my Christmas Eve preparations in March! I no sooner get the reindeer in the stables and the red suit in the cedar chest, when I have to start planning all over again.

My biggest gripe comes from having to meet all the regulations created by your societies. It was so much simpler when there were just a few empires ruling everything. There was none of this getting bounced around between ten different licensing departments, filling out forms in triplicate. I would simply ask each reigning monarch for permission to distribute gifts in their kingdoms and, bingo, I was on my way. Now, I have my own political action committee. It's called NOPAC, or North Pole Political Action Committee. I have three lobbyists working for me out of an office four blocks from the Capitol building. It gets expensive but, without them, I'd never be able to leave the North Pole for fear of being in violation of some rule that suddenly got enacted while nobody was looking.

Regulations, regulations, they're driving me nuts! Do you realize that your governments have actually claimed the air above their countries, and I have to get permission to fly through it? What could your leaders possibly be hiding? Don't they remember that I know when they're sleeping and awake, and when they've been bad or good? Now, to avoid being shot down over any one of a hundred different countries, I must file a flight plan with every one of them.

But, lest you believe I only have governments to deal with, I am also getting major headaches from my own labor force. This is the first time I've ever discussed it, but we almost didn't have a Christmas last year. Unknown to me, my elves organized a union. They call themselves the International Brotherhood of Elfin Toymakers, and last November they threatened to strike.

Their demands were that they should get paid for making toys and receive full medical and dental benefits. I reminded them that, being elves, they never get sick or old so they don't need benefits. As for being paid, I told them that North Pole Industries couldn't meet their demands, because we don't charge for the presents I deliver. Finally, I convinced them of my dilemma and we agreed that, on a yearly basis, I will replace their worn-out green tights and pointy shoes.

Well, their contentment didn't last long. This year the elves are ready to strike again because now they don't want to make wooden toys and cloth dolls anymore. They think I should institute a job training program because they want to learn high-tech skills, so they can manufacture fancy electronic toys. If this keeps up, I might have to outsource the work.

Wait, though, there's more. My insurance premiums have skyrocketed, I am facing complaints of unfair competition from Federal Express and UPS, I have been screamed at, shot at, mugged, my lungs are going bad from flying through all the air pollution, and what really gets my goat, I am being sued for 13.5 million dollars by Bruce and Bernice Tatertot.

The thrust of the lawsuit is that their son Byron is terribly upset that he didn't receive all the Christmas gifts he wanted. His parents feel that, because of Byron's distress, he will never live up to his potential. The 13.5 million is compensation for lost earnings since, according to Bruce and Bernice, Byron was destined to become a brilliant doctor. The argument made by my lawyer, that Byron's 1.04 grade point average and his frequent disrespect towards adults were the reasons he didn't get everything he wanted, is being challenged by the Tatertots' lawyer. The Tatertots feel that 300 years of tradition is irrelevant and I should have had a signed contract stating that "Byron's Christmas rewards are based on his performance during the 364 days preceding said holiday."

I have reached the end of my patience. It's time for me and Mrs. Claus to retire to a tiny Caribbean island I spotted during one of my trips. I am sick of the Arctic cold, nights lasting six months, regulations, complaints, ungrateful parents, and snooty kids. I want to kick back and enjoy some sun, golf, and deep-sea fishing while I still have life in me. So don't be surprised if, on some Christmas Eve, not all the gifts get delivered in one night. It'll mean that I have finally found my replacement and that person hasn't learned the route yet.

Regards,
Santa

David Sabbagh

Just Say No

Hi, my name's Dave. Looking at me, you'd think I lead a very plain life. Unfortunately, it's been anything but plain. You see, I am an addict. This ad•dik•shun hasn't been covered in the news media because it's not ek•si•ting. There are no gun battles or drive-by shootings, and the dealers don't carry Uzis and kill people who don't pay their debts. Hell, the people who make this stuff are even ad•ver•tie•sing it on TV and selling it to parents. I bought it and now, damnit, I'm hooked on phonics!

It all started about five months ago when I saw this nice teacher on TV, telling me that this was the best way to teach kids to read. My son, Phillip, was falling behind in his reading class, so I decided to buy the course. After it arrived, I began to help Phillip use phonics to sound out words so that he could read by himself. Before I knew it, I began sounding out words myself. It was an intense rush to be able to pro•noun•se any big word I came across. I couldn't stop. I needed more so, I started going to the library on weekends and reading si•in•ti•fik journals on bye•o•kem•is•tree, klin•i•kall si•kol•o•gee, and kul•churall an•throw•pol•o•gee. Anything that had big words in it.

After a month, sounding out words at the library wasn't enough. I did it at parties, in front of our friends. My wife became so m•bare•ass•ed she gave me an ul•ti•may•tum, either her or the fo•ne•tiks. She and the kids are now at her parents. Even her leaving didn't matter. I was sounding out every po•lee•sill•a•bik word I came across. Then, I hit rock bottom. I did fo•ne•tiks during work. At first, I would do it quietly in my q•bi•call. Ee•ven•chu•al•lee I took my newspaper to the restroom and spent 10, 20, even 40 minutes sounding out words. My ko•work•ers never knew I was hooked on phonics until one day, during an im•por•tant pree•sen•ta•shun, I sounded out the text I was dee•liv•er•ing to the ah•ten•dees. My boss, and my boss' boss were there. That was the last straw. I was called into my boss' office and given an ek•sten•dead medical leave.

I am slowly ree•kov•er•ing. I try and take it one day at a time, but it's tough. I'm not able to read any adult material yet, but I can handle Dr. Seuss and Curious George. My wife and the kids are back, but she is still hes•i•tent to begin a kon•ver•sa•shun. We still don't have a social life. There's no way I could possibly read the menu at our favorite Italian rest•aw•rawnt like I used to. We are limited to carry-out pizza. The doctors think I can completely recover, but it won't happen until my kids are reading on their own. This has been tough on me and my family. I sometimes wish we lived in a less kom•pli•ca•ted society where things could be described using words with no more than two sill•a•bells. Then reading wouldn't be so diff•i•kult. Oh well, I know I'll recover but until then, at least there's TV.

Bartering

Carl and Sandy made their way past the cluttered wooden stalls that lined the sidewalks of Nogales, Mexico. The vendors, calling from their stalls to the many tourists, and the blaring horns of the old cars and brightly painted school buses that crowded the streets filled the air with an endless flood of noise. The day was bright and the temperature pleasant.

"I can't believe I let you talk me into giving up my Saturday to come to this dumpy town," said Carl. "There are a hundred other things I could be doing at the office or around the house. Besides, it smells like garbage, and I'm getting dirty from all the dust in the air."

"Oh, don't be so boring," said Sandy, "we never do anything together, and I thought it'd be fun for us to do a little shopping and then go to dinner."

"Shopping!? All I see here are dozens of street vendors selling cheesy Mexican trinkets that we'd never use."

"I don't know about that, Carl. I think some of these things are adorable. Look, here, what an interesting teapot. It's a little white elephant, and its trunk is the spout."

"Come on, Sandy, do you really think anybody would use something like that?"

"Yes, I do," said Sandy, moving forward with a bounce perfected during her cheerleading days in college. "Let's ask that old man how much he wants for it."

"Wait a second," growled Carl, grabbing Sandy's arm with a large hand that was once used to throw touchdown passes, but is now used only to carry a briefcase. "Don't you know anything about these vendors? They think *sucker* when they see an American coming and, if you don't barter with them, you'll get ripped off. Let me do the talking."

"Hey buddy," said Carl authoritatively to an elderly man with a dark, weathered complexion and kindly eyes.

"Yes, Señor, what I do for you?"

"How much for this?" asked Carl, pointing at the small teapot that had caught his wife's interest.

"For you, Señor, 15 dollars."

"What? That's outrageous! It probably doesn't even hold two cups of tea."

"But Señor, it is handmade using the finest porcelain. And look at the bright colors of the harness across the elephant's back. It is a work of art," the elderly man said proudly.

"Art my ass, I could buy a teapot that's twice the size for a third of the price," said Carl condescendingly.

"Carl," said Sandy "don't be so mean to him. It is painted nicely, and I really like it."

"Jesus, Sandy, don't let him hear you say things like that," Carl whispered forcefully. "He'll never drop his price if he thinks you really like it."

"Come on, Carl, we can afford it and this man surely doesn't have much money."

"Forget it, I'm not paying 15 dollars for that piece of junk."

After quietly listening to Carl's hostile comments, the old man said, "Señor, you no see how much your lovely wife wants the teapot? There is no price too big to make her happy."

"Ah, she'll live without it."

"Señor, this teapot also make magic."

"Come on, what kind of crap is that?"

"Really Señor, this teapot can make magic happen."

"Carl, can't we buy it from this poor man. He's been so nice to us."

"Sorry, we don't want it."

As Carl turned to walk away, the old man said "Wait, I make a deal with you."

"See," Carl whispered, "I know how to deal with these sneaky vendors. I knew he would drop his price. They're all alike."

"Señor, I tell you what I do. For you, the teapot is still 15 dollars. But for your wife, the teapot is a gift from me. Such a woman as your wife should never be sad."

Sandy stood there beaming as the kindly vendor handed her his magic teapot, and Carl stalked off down the street.

David Sabbagh

Supersaturation

Supersaturation is a term used in the field of chemistry to describe a process of formation. Another process, that can be described using supersaturation, is the creative process.

Supersaturation occurs when there is more of a compound, called a salt, dissolved in a liquid than is naturally possible. A supersaturated solution is created by slowly dissolving a salt into a heated liquid, then letting the solution cool. The glass container used to hold the solution must be perfectly free of dirt or any other impurities that would inhibit the salt from completely dissolving.

The magical property of a supersaturated solution is that it remains clear and still until the slightest disturbance, such as a person touching the container wall or a tiny speck of dust landing on the surface of the solution, causes the atoms of the salt to furiously combine, forming a crystal inside the container. The crystal's growth follows no set pattern; each atom is free to bond to whatever neighboring atom it encounters. As the atoms bond to one another, sides form, lines appear, and corners emerge. How the crystal will look cannot be determined until the dissolved salt has been used up.

The creative process can be likened to supersaturation. Our mind is the container of liquid. As we move through life, words, visions, sounds, and experiences dissolve in our mind, causing it to become supersaturated. We continue along our path involving ourself in life's necessary activities until, one day, something happens to disturb the supersaturated solution of words, sights, and sounds. The event might be something we see or hear. It could be the smell of someone's perfume or of food being cooked. Whatever the disturbance, it has the effect of being the seed that causes all of our stored thoughts, ideas, and experiences to crystallize into something concrete and tangible, like a poem, a piece of fiction, a song, even a presentation for work.

For our mind to support this sudden creation, it must be free of the fear of making a mistake. We cannot possess any self-consciousness that might inhibit the free-forming of ideas into something whole, just as any impurities would inhibit the formation of the crystal. As the crystal grows into some unpredictable form, likewise the words, sounds, or images in our mind take on unexpected shapes, only revealing themselves as we express them through our writing, or painting, or music. Those of us who write know that feeling when we are not really thinking of creating a work but we hear or see something and, suddenly, an entire poem or story comes pouring out of our mind.

This crystallization occurred for me while I was thinking about a dream I had. As I mulled over the meaning of the dream, I realized that it was so surreal I had no hope of deciphering it. One thought led to another and the instant a particularly humorous one entered my mind, the following poem crystallized:

Indecipherable Dreams

They say answers can be found in dreams.
I hope so, I think,
as I fall into a slumber.

Do you remember me? says the attractive woman
behind the counter at the tennis club.
Sure, you wouldn't go out with me
when I asked.

The two-masted schooner with me aboard,
clinging to the rigging,
fights to survive in a stormy sea.
Through relentless waves crashing over the side,
I see a woman in a lifeboat.
The schooner moves in the opposite direction.

I arrive at Tuba City,
a small town in no place in particular.
I inquire of a local teenager,
Where did you get the sub sandwich?
At a rock opera, is his reply.

David Sabbagh

I receive my sub sandwich,
provided by TubaWayToGo,
and find a seat.

The lead character,
face painted white,
lips crimson red,
black hair, clothes, and eyes,
sings the final aria.
None of his words reach my ears.

Bewildered, I stare into space
wondering why my dream mind
is so reluctant to reveal
what I need.

I believe we all can benefit from the process of supersaturation.
We need only be aware of our surroundings and then be receptive of
the ideas which suddenly crystallize in our minds.

○

The warming rays of the sun,
bathe my upturned face.
You are my friend.

Polly Opsahl
Having a Great Time Wish You Were Here

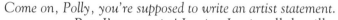

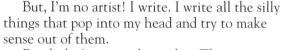

Come on, Polly, you're supposed to write an artist statement.

But, I'm no artist! I write. I write all the silly things that pop into my head and try to make sense out of them.

People don't want to know that! They want to know your driving force, what makes you tick, where you're coming from.

I come from Rochester, Michigan. I drive a Saturn. And, my watch is broken.

People want to know where you get your ideas and what kind of writing you do. In fact, they really want to know why you write at all.

I'm not sure I know where my ideas come from. Sometimes, I hear a word or part of a song, and a picture just pops into my head. Other times, an idea or phrase sets off a chain reaction in my mind, like a string of firecrackers. As for why I write, well . . . I can't paint or draw. I've always just found it easier to express myself in writing.

Now, what type of writing do you do and why?

Nearing my fortieth birthday, I had about twenty chapters of an unfinished novel, and several half-written stories. Before I found myself decades older carrying around a big neon *if only* sign, I decided it was time to get serious about my writing. I signed up for a creative writing class and announced that I couldn't *do* poetry. I've been writing poems ever since.

Polly Opsahl

Adrift in the Universe

The day is old. A ruddy sun
sits on the horizon like the head
of a bald man with no neck and high
blood pressure,

bathing trunks, patterned with forests
and rivers, cover his protruding earth belly
as he floats on the midnight blue universal tide.

He spins around and around and around in a whirlpool
of existence. Puffy hands paddle with effort,
but never alter his direction. And still

he paddles. His legs move
as if to frog kick. One moon
knee rises as his head drops
below the horizon. Toes
and fingernails twinkle
like stars. He
wonders
how long
he can
stay afloat.

Polly Opsahl

Hunting Season

A corkscrew willow stands
at one end of a clearing,
looking like a wild queen
on her throne. Her thin
leafless branches tangle,
flowing strands of hair
tossed by north winds.

Her trunk and roots spread,
tattered hem of a trailing gown.
Squirrels and birds, loyal subjects,
seek shelter within her realm,
pay homage lest they be
flung to the ground in a fit
of bad weather. Pine trees sway

their curtsies, ladies-in-waiting
to rule the meadow, should Majesty
topple from her throne. A deer prince
lies at her feet, antler crown askew.
Emptied, eyes turn to her in supplication.
She sees his entreaty, can do nothing
but weep. Blood pools on pine carpet.

The hunter enters her audience,
usurper of power, scepter smoking.

Polly Opsahl

The Song, the Chair, and the Sea

Opal sits in a bentwood rocker, cradles a newborn babe. Looking out at the pounding surf, tired eyes forget more than they remember. Her soft flesh is wrinkled, as if every minute of life drains part of her from between skin and bone. The child is just as soft, just as wrinkled, but empty, as if in anticipation, as if waiting to be filled. Opal rocks in rhythm with the sea, keeps time by the clack of runner against worn wood floor. She lifts her hand and then presses it against the baby's back as they roll forward, roll back and lift, roll forth and press. The infant sleeps, face nestled in Opal's shoulder; her bulky sweater provides the cushion her wasted body lacks. While Opal softly hums the lullabies of mermaids, two hearts keep time with the song, the chair, and the sea. As the child wakes, new eyes open, knowing more than they will ever forget. Her murmurs mingle with Opal's voice, create music as fresh as a wave, as old as the sand, as new as the wind. In the quiet between sunset and moonrise, the sea calms; the tide envelops the shore; their duet ends. Opal shifts the baby in her weary arms; old eyes flow into new. Rising, she lays the child in a rough-hewn cradle that sits near the rocker, bends to kiss a velvet cheek. The infant fixes Opal's faded blue eyes with her own, the color of a storm-tossed sea.

Polly Opsahl

Body Language

Face down in the pool, immersed
in chlorinated water, my arms
move in a steady Australian crawl.
I feel the pull of your eyes
through the back of my head. Like

a red-beamed laser, they slice
painlessly through flesh, bone,
and tissue. Water rushes in
my ears, your pulse beats
cadence into my swim

through life. Your body speaks
in a language not of words,
every cell in discordant harmony
with the current of my soul.

Polly Opsahl

On the Ribbon of His Voice

In a hospital bed crowded
by people and machines he doesn't know,
he watches her. A stark white sheet
tucked under her chin declares

in bold black letters, ST. JOSEPH'S MERCY,
the HOSPITAL barely visible as if the hands
of too many dying patients clutched
that one spot in their last attempt

to hold on to life, or in their final
unspoken prayer. Her blue eyes speak
to him of pain and fear. He wonders
if she can read the same in his.

A kind nurse shows him how to reach
through cords and tubes to touch her hand.
She grabs his with a strength that defies
her fading body. He smiles briefly, blinks back

tears, and wills her not to let go of life, of him.
He bends to speak into her ear to be heard
above the voices of nurses, machines.
He whispers of love and their life together,

not wanting strangers or death
to intrude on intimate memories. He talks
of joy at the birth of a son, shared
laughter at his silly jokes, nights

of little sleep and much passion. The specters
of death and attendants fade for a time
as they travel through their life together
on the ribbon of his voice. As the hours

pass, his throat dries and cracks, but he
pushes on, unwilling to end the journey
too soon. As night envelops the outside
world, they remain isolated in a pool

of soft light from above her bed.
Except for one to share his vigil,
the doctors and nurses leave to attend
other patients. Death waits for her outside

the light, anticipates her oncoming invitation.
Her blue eyes seem less bright and less
blue as he tries to read her thoughts. He senses
a plea for forgiveness and release. He stands,

turns out the light. She catches his tears
in the palm of her still hand.

Polly Opsahl

Laura Gail

Less than a year older,
Laura Gail lived next door.
A black and white photo dated
1959 shows us on my swing set.

She wears a short pleated skirt,
white blouse with peter pan collar,
and lace socks folded precisely
to meet the edge of her black
patent leather Mary Janes.
The tiniest, straightest barrette
holds her shoulder length hair
off to one side. I wear

hand-me-downs from my sister,
mismatched shorts and a stupid
sleeveless top. My pixie cut hair
sticks out at odd angles from cowlicks
on each side of my forehead.
Laura Gail smiles at the camera;
I smile at Laura Gail.

I learned about Barbie dolls
and boys from Laura Gail.
At her house, I tasted my first
slice of American cheese. She
taught me how to break it
into square bits, hold it
on my tongue and let it melt,
sweet and creamy.

Dreamlord

I enter my apartment house of dreams,
each resident a part of my now, my then, my when.
Debbie Reynolds lives in 36-D; she pops in
every few months to borrow another cup of sugar.
I wonder where she keeps it all? I visit
my dead grandparents on the fourth floor
every Wednesday. My children
and my husband move from room to room,
often waiting just beyond an open door
or down the hall around the corner. Some nights,

I stay in one place, have coffee with my mother;
others, I wander hallways never certain
of my destination. I climb stairs to meet familiar
faces I don't know, or step down, down to find
sides of myself I'd rather not recognize.
The elevator can shoot to Neptune or plummet
into night terrors of mirrors with no reflections
and monsters who live next door. Inner doors

lead to my kitchen or Las Vegas. Outer doors
take me to next week's meeting or Christmas, 1967.
Windows stick open on painful memories
of lost friendships, forgotten birthdays, drunken fathers.
Harsh words I wish never spoken follow me
when I wake, haunt me like notes of rent past due.

Polly Opsahl

The Dead and Roses

Through a dream garden I walk. My dead mother
paints lilacs, impatiens, bleeding hearts
in vivid purple hues. A ballerina
weather vane dances north
past trillium and myrtle.

My mother and the ballerina become one,
pull me down a path past morning
glory and tiger lily to my own
backyard. There, a bush
doubles over

with the weight of one hundred roses.
I pluck a blood red blossom, cradle
it in my two palms. Fragrance
fills my lungs as the petals
begin to throb.

Warm mist beads on the surface. In my hand
beats a human heart. With wonder I look
into my mother's face. She fades.
The pulsating heart I hold
stills, becomes

a rose with petals wilted, dry, fragile. The bush
stands empty, no blossoms, no leaves.
I wake in my bed, cold beads of sweat
at my brow. Beneath my breast
my heart pounds.

On my white satin pillowcase
three fresh rose petals,
blood red.

Haunted

By the icy water of Lake Huron she feels
the warmth of his hand on her arm
as if to say, *Stop. Look at that cloud,*
that bird, that light on the water. Clouds
change shape in the wind from a frog,
to a flower, to a castle. Seagulls glide,
dive, search the water's surface
for the glint of their next meal. Sunbeams
sprinkle diamonds on the waves. She turns
to share her delight, but he's not there.

On a mountaintop in the Grand Canyon
she closes her eyes. He warms her in spring
sunshine. Her hat falls to the ground
as his fingers comb through her hair
with the wind. She raises her arms
for an embrace and feels the flutter
of a kiss on her lips as she hugs
the air. Her hat topples off the edge, tumbles
end over end over end, disappears.

She stands before the antique floor mirror
in the bedroom, holds her faded wedding gown
against her still-thin body. She sees
his desire, watches his arms encircle
her waist from behind, feels his warm breath
on her neck. She raises her hand to touch
his cheek but he's not there. Their eyes
lock in the mirror. She can't turn away.
Drawn toward him, she steps
into the glass, takes him in her arms.

The gown drifts to the floor like snow.

Polly Opsahl

Bluebird Outside My Window

In the still of just past midnight, I dream of songbirds.
Chickadee whistles my name; noisy fox sparrow tells
the coming of winter. In skylark's melody I hear
the clear blue of ocean, the green of meadow, the brown
of desert sand rippling across dunes. The mournful
coo of a dove echoes in my heart cries of the silenced.

Carolina parakeet, Santa Barbara song sparrow were silenced
by deforestation, destruction of trees and bushes these birds
called home. Labrador duck. Heath hen. Does no one mourn
their absence? My grandfather, as the boy I never knew, tells
of millions of passenger pigeons coloring the sky brown
with their passing. The gaudy scarlet tanager hears

the victims; their cries echo repeatedly in his short song. I hear
fear of humans who, in only three hundred years, silenced
one of the most abundant species ever on earth. Bald eagles, brown
pelicans, California condors, yellow-shouldered blackbirds
are threatened, endangered by pesticides and nest predation. *Tell
me, promise me, it's not too late*, sings the nightingale each morning.

A purple martin washes herself, sips dew from the cup of a morning
glory until the European starling pushes her aside. No mate hears
its courtship melody; dusky seaside sparrow succumbs. Telltale
signs of human indifference hush the waterfowl; doomed to silence,
oil spills on the western grebes. The ruby-throated hummingbird's
wings beat waterfall rhythms on glistening boulders browned

in riverbeds of time. Common grackle's song is less harsh. Brown
thrasher repeats twice each horrific loss of habitat, mourning
for rain forests, wetlands and the pink-headed duck, first bird
to fall victim to people reclaiming land they never owned. Here
go yellow-billed cuckoos and short-eared owls. Almost silent
now, the black tern and Kirtland's warbler search for stars to tell

their stories to. But city lights extinguish fireflies and stars, tell
the moon to fade away. Wood thrush holds his brown
head erect as his dramatic call rings through a world more silent.
The swan stands mute. Red robin's breast stills. Doves mourn
as acid rain falls on the harlequin duck. I listen and hear
wings of the past as the melodious song of the mockingbird

drifts through and breaks the silence of almost mourning.
I wake to a future that tells of the past. Contamination's brown
foams at water's edge. I hear feathers break on the bluebird.

Polly Opsahl

Waiting Outside the Divorce Lawyer's Office

In a brief respite from cold,
January-in-Detroit gloom, sunlight
streams through my Taurus windshield,
mixes with recirculated heat
that blasts on high. Parched skin craves
my last drop of cocoa butter lotion
as I wait, basking in daybright rare
in overcast Michigan sky.

Steamy air hangs thick and moist,
like Florida in August. I close my eyes,
remember Flamingo Cove and you.
Scratchy wool becomes white beach
sandpapering bare flesh. The sun
touches my cheeks unfiltered
through safety glass, warm breezes
caress my face from the Gulf

instead of dashboard vents. You
massage suntan oil over my back,
my legs. Water dances in the fountain
outside our cabana; melting icicles
drip on icy steps leading
to the end of our marriage.

D.P.W. Man

Detroit Public Works comes to my door wearing
tight green pants, a light green long-sleeved shirt,
and heavy boots caked with mud in assorted colors

and wet. Sleeves rolled past his elbows reveal
tan arms, and a white patch over his pocket
introduces him in red embroidery as Lance.
His callused hand points to a spot in my front yard.

He tells me my main line is cracked, and I'm leaking
out into the street. Water bubbles up amid a circle
of dandelions, as if they anticipate and celebrate
this dance of freedom from earth and cast iron.

He says my pressure is dangerously high and,
left untended, the line could rupture, and I would
really have a mess to contend with.
You wouldn't want that, would ya, lady?

He details the possible destruction and mud
that would result if I don't allow him to
invade my yard immediately with his backhoe.
I watch the dazzle of droplets on grassy blades,

notice how much greener they look than the rest
of the parched lawn, and consider my option
to let the water flow unrestrained. Can I accept
the consequences of unbridled release?

Go ahead, I say. The D.P.W. man grins;
his teeth shine white against brown skin. I glimpse
the glistening stream in his sea green eyes,
close the door, and turn the faucet on, cold.

Polly Opsahl

Without You

I am January in Florida,
not very warm, not really cold,
brown and bare, a palm tree
teetering on a deserted beach.

Without you I am February
in Michigan. Winds howl
off Great Lakes. My climate
changes overnight from freezing
sunshine to a balmy winter thaw.
Snow drifts on my door, blows
through cracks in my insulation.

I am St. Patrick's Day at the corner bar,
rowdy and unruly. I look for any excuse
to have another drink. I see you
in every face, drown my sorrows
in a glass of green beer. Without

you I am an April fool, a maypole
on the moon with ribbons
limp in airless disinterest.
A groomless June bride, I stand
at empty altars. Without you

I am a dud in the box
of 4th of July fireworks,
a cat in a week
of August dog days.

I labor through each hour.
I yearn to set sail
in search of New Worlds.
I am a disabled veteran
in a war of emotions.

Without you, I am a string
of unlit Christmas lights,
the count down to a New Year
where every second feels like

January in Florida, not very warm,
not really cold, brown and bare,
a palm tree teetering on a deserted beach.

Polly Opsahl

Thief

for Tammy

No one notices amid the neon
and dazzle of Starlight Casino,
one more sparkle, one more gleam,
as he releases the switchblade,
stainless steel flexed and ready,
cold and gray as his eyes.

A small blonde
slips three golden coins
into a Midas Touch machine,
as if feeding grapes to a lover.

Cradled in his hand, carved ivory
warms; he holds the knife low
and flat against his thigh.

She sets reels spinning with a pull
that makes her hair sway. A dolphin
charm swims between her shoulder blades,
suspended from a tiny braid, beaded
and six inches longer than the rest
of her natural curls.

He runs a callused thumb along the blade,
tests the sharpness.

Before the reels can stop, she slides
her hand into a plastic bucket
of tokens in her lap.

He moves to stand at her back; right
hand raises the knife.

She fingers coins, prepares
to make her next offering.

His left hand grasps the dolphin;
her head turns at the tug.

Steel blade slices fine strands
cleanly, like scissors through silk.

Her eyes never leave the machine;
three gold bars settle on the pay line.

He steals away, fondling his prize.

She screams,
Jackpot!

Polly Opsahl

Chateau d'Amore Merlot, 1973

On the edge of your mouth I sit
and contemplate my existence.
The curve of your lush lips, full
and firm, fits my body deliciously.

I repose in exquisite anxiety
awaiting your decision. Out
and back in, your tongue darts
taking bits of me to sample.

Do I compliment or clash
with your other appetites?
Am I too sweet, too dry,
the wrong color, or a perfect

accompaniment for you to savor?
I could languish here forever
and believe that I enjoy
your questionable attention.

This precipice is quite comfortable
if I remain in exactly the right spot,
the absolutely correct position.
I balance precariously

and wonder if you will
pull me inside your mouth
and swallow or spit me out
like a piece of bitter cork.

Astro-nut

Encapsulated in a rocketship of his own making,
he invades my dreams. A mere acquaintance,
I wonder at this trespass. He stands statue-still,

central star in his sheltered universe. A jaded sun
enlightened by reflected glow, he sees
himself in mirrors that spin in gravitational
rotation dance. His eyes in photos stare;
his face revolves with adoration frozen
and framed in glass. He traps me

into reluctant orbit with *I want* and *I need.*
His demands drag me down, pull me
too close. I risk being consumed
if I fail to gain escape velocity.
Breaking away,

I become a shooting star.

Polly Opsahl

Having a Great Time Wish You Were Here

My pink flamingo lawn ornament
leaves me. All that remains
are two pencil-thin leg holes

in the backyard next to the azalea.
At first, I think he's been kidnapped,
but when I receive no ransom note,

I realize he's run away. I wait
by the phone, sure he'll call remorseful
over making me worry. I hear nothing

until a postcard arrives
from London. *Decided it was time
to see the world. Couldn't wait for you*

any longer. Love, Butch.
The next day, another drops
through the mail slot, the kind

with the sender in the picture. Butch
stands in front of the Eiffel Tower
wearing a beret and a striped shirt

that shows off his pink chest.
Cards arrive daily. I get two
or three at a time: Butch

at a bullfight in Spain,
outside the Taj Mahal, strolling
through Red Square, snorkeling

in the Great Barrier Reef, sunbathing
on a topless beach in the Mediterranean,
all the places we planned to visit together

someday. The backyard seems strange
without Butch. In the garden,
a family of ants moves into his leg holes.

About the Writers

Margo LaGattuta, editor, is a poet with four published books: *Embracing the Fall* (Plain View Press), *The Dream Givers* (Lake Shore Publishing), *No Edge Lines* (Earhart Press) and *Diversion Road* (State Street Press). This is the second Plain View Press anthology she has edited. The first, *Variations on the Ordinary*, was published in 1995. She has an MFA from Vermont College, teaches writing at Oakland Community College, and hosts a weekly radio interview program. Her poems and essays have appeared in many literary magazines and presses.

John Milam is a writer and health care worker dealing with Traumatic Brain Injury (TBI) and other life challenges. He has been writing professionally since 1994, and he is presently working on a book about life after Traumatic Brain Injury. His writing has appeared in *Touchstone Journal*.

Bethany Irene Schryburt, a Rochester, Michigan, school bus driver, earned her BA in English at Wayne State University (Detroit) in 1995 and will soon complete an MA in Creative Writing. She is editor of *Van Dyke Quarterly*, a Ford Motor Company publication. While living in Canada, she wrote and directed *Yarns to Spin*, winning an *Ontario Bicentennial Award* in 1984. She has won *Tompkins Awards* for both fiction and drama from Wayne State University.

Poems by **Mike Jones** have appeared in *HalfTones to Jubilee*, *Mobius*, *Zuzu's Petals Quarterly*, *The Cathartic*, and other journals. He is a real estate broker, appraiser and consultant by profession, also a business owner, teacher, and father of three. He has an MA in English Literature from Oakland University and a BA in Communications and English from University of Michigan.

Linda K. Sienkiewicz has exhibited artwork and taught calligraphy in Cleveland, Ohio and in Michigan, where she now lives. She designs and sews clothing and accessories. Her poems have appeared in *Muddy River Poetry Review*, *Kumquat Meringue*, *The Poetic Soul*, and *Poet's Coffeehouse Quarterly*. Linda finds much support and camaraderie with on-line poets and is a member of the AOL Writer's Club Poetry Workshop.

Mary-Jo Lord has a Master's degree in counseling and works at Oakland Community College as an Academic Support Coordinator. Her writing has been printed in publications by The National Library of Poetry and The National Federation of the Blind Writers Division. She uses the pen name M.J. Lord.

Lori Solymosi, visual artist and poet, graduated from Pennsylvania Academy of Fine Arts, where she received the Emlen Cresson Traveling Award. The former director and founding member of The North Penn Arts Alliance in Pennsylvania, she also graduated from University of Massachusetts Arts Extension Services in Arts Management. She teaches art to children and adults at the Birmingham Bloomfield Art Association and exhibits in area galleries.

Karen Renaud is a mom, writer, teacher, perpetual student and local zoning official. She and her husband Jim have four children and two daughters-in-law. She owns an accounting proprietorship and co-owns Ace Controls, Inc. A member of the Clicking Bones Writer's Group, she also edits newsletters and has spent fifteen years as secretary of various boards of directors. Her writing has been published in *Speakeasy Journal*, *The Blues Review* and *The Eccentric* newspapers.

Anita Elaine Page is a retired elementary school principal living in Rochester Hills, Michigan. She started writing in 1991 and has been published in *The Mature American*, *Abbey*, *Womenwise* and *Parnassus Literary Journal*. She is a member of the United Amateur Press Association of America and has served as U.A.P.A.A. Critic for three years.

Linda Angér attended Oakland Community College and Western Michigan University, majoring in creative writing. She was editor of *Living the HAIlife*, a newsletter for the Human Awareness Institute of Michigan. She's had a love affair with poetry all her life, and her work has appeared in *la Journal Français d'Amerique*, *PhenomeNEWS*, *Touchstone Journal*, *Freedom Writer's Unite* and others. A member of the Clicking Bones Writer's Group, she lives with her son Ethan Flick in Auburn Hills, Michigan.

David Sabbagh has always had a predisposition for words, but it wasn't until 1992 that he started seriously writing. His prose has been published in *MetroTimes* and *Touchstone Journal*. He is currently employed in the computer services field.

Polly Opsahl is a letter carrier and Union activist. She began taking creative writing classes again almost twenty years after attending Michigan State University and discovered a love of poetry. She writes regularly for *New Vision*, a Union newsletter, and is currently serving as its editor.